POSSE FROM POISON CREEK

The minute Sheriff Webb Dolan led the posse out of town he knew he was in serious trouble. The three murdering outlaws were already hours into the deadly Ute Indian country . . . and some of Dolan's recruits were unfit to go after them. Worse yet, Dolan realized, his fellow lawman Floyd Aragon had no intention of actually capturing the badmen. He might cut them all down like dogs and grab the stolen money for himself. And what would he do to the beautiful woman who had joined their band?

In the middle of the sun-baked desert there was bound to be a blood-drenched showdown!

POSSE FROM
POISON CREEK

Lewis B. Patten

GUNSMOKE

First published in the UK by Mayflower Books

This hardback edition 2008
by BBC Audiobooks Ltd
by arrangement with
Golden West Literary Agency

ISBN 978 1 405 68160 5

British Library Cataloguing in Publication Data available.

Printed and bound in Great Britain by
Antony Rowe Ltd., Chippenham, Wiltshire

CHAPTER ONE

Webb Dolan was sheriff of Plateau County, Colorado. He was a big, rangy, patient man, given to thoughtful speech, inclined to give his fellow men the benefit of the doubt whenever possible. He was occasionally called upon to break up a fight or jail a drunk, but mostly his job nowadays consisted of serving legal papers for the court.

That was his errand in Pagosa today. He pulled his sweating horse to a halt at the top of the sagebrush-covered ridge east of town and stared at the road winding down, at the town lying at the bottom of the ridge, drowsing in the late afternoon sun.

Beyond the town, Poison Creek, swollen from the cloudburst on its upper reaches, twisted back and forth, finally emptying into the river and muddying it for a mile below. Pagosa's two principal streets were Main and Elm, and they crossed in front of the bank.

The bank was the most substantial building in town. Built of brick, it bore a sign over its door, "Bank of Pagosa," and it existed to serve the needs of the ranchers within a twenty-five-mile radius.

Dolan fished a sack of tobacco from his pocket and rolled a cigarette. He licked it, put it into his mouth, thumbed a match alight and inhaled absently. He was thinking about Floyd Aragon, town marshal of Pa-

1

gosa, and wondering where he was today. He didn't like Floyd Aragon. He hoped he wouldn't have to see him or talk to him. Aragon was officious and pompous and arrogant. He expected the sheriff to check in with him every time he came to town.

Three horses were tied in front of Calvin Daybright's store. Three men came out of the adjoining saloon that Daybright operated in conjunction with the store. They stood for a moment in front, and Dolan saw a cloud of tobacco smoke rise from one of them as he lighted a pipe or a cigar. They untied their horses and walked to the corner in front of the bank.

Uneasiness touched the sheriff briefly, but he scoffed at it. Nothing ever happened nowadays. Nothing was going to happen down there this afternoon. Not with him sitting here watching it.

A girl in a bright blue dress that could only be Calvin Daybright's little seven-year-old, Susan, came walking along the street from the direction of her house. She stopped to pet a dog lying in the shade.

Two of the three men went into the bank. The third remained outside, holding the horses' reins.

For the first time, Dolan felt real alarm. But he didn't get excited and he didn't move. Even if the bank was being robbed, he couldn't reach it in time to do anything about it. On the other hand, if he stayed here, he could at least see which way the robbers went.

It was like watching a play unfold on stage. He heard the faint popping of guns, and he saw the two men run out of the bank. One carried several white canvas sacks. The other had a gun in his hand. They seized the reins of their horses from the third man, who had been holding them, mounted and whirled away toward the north.

A man came running out of the bank. Smoke

puffed from a rifle in his hands. It was an instant before the report reached Dolan's ears. In that instant he saw Susan Daybright get to her feet and run across the street toward her father's store.

The three galloping horses raced toward her. Dolan's fists were clenched, his breath held anxiously. He whispered, "Oh God. . . !" but his prayer came too late. The three horses swept over the little girl, and when they had gone, she lay still in the middle of the street, a spot of bright blue against the tan-colored dust. Again smoke puffed from the rifle of the man in front of the bank, and this time one of the bank robbers swayed in his saddle. He recovered, righted himself and raced after the other two. The three took the road that followed Poison Creek north toward the towering sandstone cliffs of the Ute Plateau.

Characteristically, Webb Dolan made his assessment of the situation immediately, even as he kneed his horse down the twisting road toward town. The three had obviously planned the robbery well. They had planned it for late afternoon, knowing they could stay ahead of any pursuit that might develop until after dark. Since no one could trail them in the dark, they would, by morning, have an eight-hour lead.

It was now nearly five o'clock. In another ten minutes the bank would have been closed. The robbers had undoubtedly known that, too.

Having planned this well, Webb knew they would also have mapped their route out of the valley of Poison Creek, across the Ute Plateau and on to whatever their destination was. They would have planned on leaving the road shortly after dark. By doing so, they would make sure they could not be followed by trackers or caught by a posse trying to outguess them by blindly following the road up Poison Creek to the trail at its head.

At this time of year it got dark at eight. That meant the outlaws would have three hours of riding before they could leave the road. Three hours of hard riding would put them at the Horse Ridge Trail. But Webb knew that didn't mean the Horse Ridge Trail was the one they'd take. They'd circle through the sagebrush for an hour or so after dark before taking any route, thus confusing the pursuit as to whether they had taken the Horse Ridge Trail or continued up the valley of Poison Creek or doubled back toward town.

A crowd had gathered around the spot of bright blue lying in the street. There was another crowd in front of the bank. Neither crowd was big. There were only a hundred and seventeen people living in the town.

Dolan was a quarter mile away. He kept his horse at a steady trot. As the road descended, trees and houses obscured his view of the happenings in front of the bank. He rode down Elm between rows of young elm trees and at last reached the bank.

All was confusion. People stood on the boardwalks, talking in subdued, excited tones. Susan Daybright was gone.

Webb Dolan swung stiffly from his horse. He tied the reins to the rail in front of the bank, took off his hat and wiped his forehead with a hand. Miles Dunklee ran excitedly from the bank. "Jesus Christ, Webb, I'm glad you're here! Three men just held me up! They'd have killed me if I hadn't ducked down behind the counter there! They—"

Dolan interrupted. "What about Susan Daybright? It was her they ran down, wasn't it?"

Dunklee nodded, his expression sober. "She's dead, Webb. Cal just carried her home in his arms."

Half a dozen men now crowded around Webb. "You're going to organize a posse, ain't you, Webb?"

Dolan looked at Dunklee. "How much did they get?"

Dunklee's flabby face was almost gray, and a film of sweat covered it. He looked as though he was going to be sick. He shook his head dazedly. "I can't tell exactly without some figuring, but it was a lot. Maybe seven or eight thousand dollars." He dragged out a white handkerchief and mopped his face with it. "Hadn't you better get going, Webb? They'll get a start...."

Dolan asked, "Where's Aragon?"

"He and some others went after horses at the livery. They're going after the holdup men."

A man yelled, "What good does it do to stand here talking about it? Susan Daybright is dead. Those crooks have got seven or eight thousand dollars they took from the bank. Talk ain't going to catch them and bring them back!"

Dolan looked at the man. "Going off half cocked won't catch them either, Hack. I was up on the ridge when they rode away. I know which way they went. I also know we'll never catch them before dark."

Floyd Aragon and three other men came galloping wildly along the street from the direction of the livery barn. Aragon yelled at them to stop, and they pulled their plunging horses to a halt in front of the bank. Aragon stared down at the sheriff and bawled, "Come on, Sheriff! We're going after them!"

Dolan shook his head. "Get down, Floyd. You've got no authority outside of town."

Aragon said a single, contemptuous, obscene word. He was a short man, broad and powerful, but going to paunch and fat. He had close-set, cruel eyes that reminded Dolan of the eyes of a boar. His mouth was thin, his neck short and thick. He shoved his hat back to reveal a sweating head that was almost bald. He turned and looked at the three men with him. "Are we going to sit here jawing, or are we going to go catch them murderers and bring them back?"

One yelled, "Let's go!"

Dolan raised his hands. He stepped out into the street. "Damn it now, wait a minute! It'll be dark in three hours. You can't go chasing off like this. I'm going to take a posse out at dawn."

Cliff Sims, one of those with Aragon, yelled, "Hell with that! We can catch them and have them in jail before you get your posse organized!"

Anger now entered Dolan's voice, "By God, I'm ordering you to stay!"

Aragon only laughed contemptuously. He whirled his horse with a brutal hand, spurred savagely and thundered up the street toward the north. The other three followed, yelling excitedly.

Dolan stared at the assembled crowd. "I want about five volunteers. I want them here at dawn, each with a good, sound horse, blankets, rifle and ammunition, a tarpaulin or slicker, food for a week and pots to cook it in. It'd be a good idea if each of you also had a change of clothes."

Miles Dunklee said, "I'm going, Webb."

Dolan studied him doubtfully. "It'll be a long, hard ride, Mr. Dunklee. We can't hold back if you get saddlesore. We'll have to leave you behind."

"It's me they robbed. I got a right. . . ."

Dolan agreed. "I guess you have. All right. Who else?"

Emmett Franks said, "I'll go."

Dolan nodded approvingly. Franks was a tall, gaunt man with skin almost the color of mahogany. He had a ranch at the head of Poison Creek, and he knew the country like the back of his hand. He was sixty-five years old, but Webb knew he could ride all day every day for a week without complaint.

Hack Grogan said, "Count me in," and Dolan nodded unenthusiastically.

There were no other volunteers. Dolan said, "Cal Daybright will probably want to go. That makes four. Where's Sam Joseph?"

A deep, drawling voice said, "Here I am, Sheriff. You want me to track for you?"

Webb turned his head. Sam Joseph was a Negro who had been born in Mississippi a slave. He was a big, powerful man between forty and forty-five. He didn't know his exact age because the records of his birth had been destroyed by the fire during the war. There wasn't a hair remaining on his head. He owned the livery stable. He had apparently heard about the holdup from Aragon and come straight here.

Dolan nodded. "We'll leave at dawn. Mr. Dunklee, Hack Grogan, Franks and Cal Daybright will be going besides you and me. I suppose Aragon and maybe a couple of those with him will want to go if they're not too played out. That'll be enough."

"Yes, sir, Sheriff." There was calm respect in Sam Joseph's tone. Dolan's eyes met those of the Negro briefly. He knew Sam Joseph to be the best tracker for a hundred miles. Sam had come West after he was emancipated at the end of the war. About twelve at the time, he had been captured by a band of Cheyennes and raised to manhood in their villages.

Sam was respectful toward all white men. But Dolan knew that hidden beneath his respectful manner was a fierce pride in himself. Sam knew he was the equal of any man, white or black. He knew he had come a long, long way, from ragged slave boy to livery-stable owner here in Pagosa, and he was proud of it.

Dolan said, "I'll see you all half an hour before

dawn." He untied his horse, mounted and rode toward Calvin Daybright's house at the upper end of Main.

It was a big, white, two-story house, the biggest and best-kept house in town. There was a cast-iron horse's-head hitching post in front, and Dolan tied his horse to it. He could hear a woman weeping as he went up the walk.

There was a twist bell on the door, but Dolan didn't use it. He knocked instead.

Cal Daybright came to the door, a tall, thin, graying man. Dolan knew that Susan had been the Daybrights' only child. He also knew they were too old to have another one.

Daybright's eyes were red, but he was calm. He said, "Hello, Webb."

Webb Dolan took off his hat and stepped into the house. He stood uneasily just inside the door. "I'm sorry, Cal. I . . . I'm sorry."

Tears appeared in Daybright's eyes. Dolan said, "I'm taking a posse out at dawn. I thought you'd want to go along."

Daybright nodded. "I want to get them, Webb. I want to get them if it's the last thing I ever do."

"We'll get them, Cal. But let's have one thing understood. We're going to bring them back for trial."

Daybright turned his pain-filled eyes on Webb. For an instant something flared in them, something wild and violent. But he nodded reluctantly.

Dolan said, "A good horse, blankets, slicker, grub. You know what to bring." He stepped out onto the porch. Turning, he said, "Give my sympathy to Mrs. Daybright, Cal."

Daybright nodded wordlessly, unable for the moment to speak. Dolan turned and walked back to his horse. He still had to serve the papers he had come here to serve, but after that he would be free to go after the men who had robbed the bank and run down helpless Susan Daybright in the street. He would be free to pursue them however long it took.

CHAPTER TWO

THE FIRST THING Dolan did was to serve the summons for which purpose he had come to town. Then he led his horse to the livery. Sam Joseph was there, and Dolan handed him the reins. "Rub him down, Sam, and give him a feed of oats. I think you'd better bring along a couple of pack horses tomorrow with about a hundred pounds of oats on each. If they're good horses, we can use them for spares when the oats are gone."

"Yes, sir, Sheriff." Sam studied him speculatively a moment. "What you goin' to do about Floyd Aragon?"

"Do? Nothing, I guess. He and the others are just wearing themselves out. They'll start the day tomorrow without sleep, and I expect that'll be trouble enough for them without me adding to it. Besides, they haven't broken any law."

He left the stable and walked along the street to the hotel, a two-story frame building that faced the bank. The crowd in front of the bank had dispersed, and the town dozed in the late afternoon sun as though nothing had happened earlier. There were two or three small groups of men sitting in the shade talking, but that wasn't unusual.

In the air now there was the smell of wood smoke,

and suddenly a smell of frying meat reminded Dolan he hadn't eaten since morning. He went into the hotel, his saddlebags slung over his shoulder, and crossed the lobby to the desk.

Luke Brodie was on duty. Dolan laid down his saddlebags, opened the register and signed his name. Brodie shoved a key at him, his expression failing to conceal his disapproval. Dolan grinned ruefully. He said, "Luke, I've been a lawman all my life. You don't catch criminals by going off half cocked, and you can't trail them in the dark. We'll get those three and bring them back for trial. But if we was to run our horses up that canyon until dark, they'd be too played out to go anywhere tomorrow."

"What if we get a storm and it wipes out all the tracks?"

Dolan said, "We won't get a storm tonight. At least it ain't likely. But even if it does rain, Sam Joseph will pick up the trail. There'll be tracks in places that are sheltered from the rain."

He turned away. The hotel had a dining room, but the food wasn't very good. Dolan always ate at Ma Ledgerwood's boarding house when he was in town. Breakfast was fifteen cents. Dinner was a quarter and supper twenty cents.

He went up to his room and laid the saddlebags on the dresser. He poured water into the basin, washed, then lathered his face and shaved. He combed his hair, put on his hat and went downstairs.

On the hotel veranda, he paused and stared up the street toward the north. In his mind, he could see Aragon and the three with him spurring their lathered horses along the road. He was certain they wouldn't catch the bank robbers. They probably wouldn't even get a glimpse of them.

They'd arrive back in town four or five hours after dark, probably around one or two o'clock. Aragon would be in an angry mood. So would the other three. The thing that would irritate Floyd Aragon most would be having to admit that the sheriff had been right.

He shrugged slightly and headed for Ma Ledgerwood's. It was a big two-story frame house on the bank of Poison Creek. The creek, swollen as it still was from the cloudburst at its headwaters yesterday, made a steady, roaring sound.

Dolan climbed the three steps to the porch and went inside. There was a large hall just inside the door, opening into a parlor, which in turn opened into the dining room.

The boarders were already taking their places at the table. Ma saw Dolan and came waddling toward him, her red, perspiring face smiling a broad welcome. "Webb! Webb Dolan! You come sit down. It's good to see you, but it's a sad thing that brought you here."

Dolan said, "I just happened to be here, Ma. I came to serve a summons."

"You goin' after them reprobates?"

He nodded. "At dawn tomorrow."

"There's them that says you should be on the road right now."

"Aragon's on the road. When he gets back, those that are grumbling will know that I was right."

He took a chair, one he knew wasn't assigned to a regular boarder. The talk around the table was excited and concerned with nothing but the robbery. One man asked Dolan, "How's Daybright taking it?"

"Hard. Susan was an only child, and they're too old to have another one."

"And Mrs. Daybright?"

"I could hear her crying."

A man muttered, "Murderers! You bring 'em back an' we'll string 'em up sure as hell."

Dolan said, "It was an accident. They didn't mean to run Susan down. I'll bring them back, but I hope some of you will have calmed down before I do."

Mrs. Ledgerwood carried in two heaping platters of meat and started them around the table. She returned to the kitchen and came back with two huge bowls, one of mashed potatoes, one of peas. These two started around the table, to be followed by gravy, hot bread, butter, strawberry preserves.

There now was little talk. The men ate swiftly and single-mindedly. When they had finished, they lighted pipes, cigars and wheat-straw cigarettes. Dolan rolled himself a smoke, then got up and went out on the porch. He could smell something fragrant blooming someplace, probably in the bed of Poison Creek, and he could hear its steady, unremitting roar.

He discovered that he didn't want to talk to any more of the townspeople about the robbery. Nobody was going to give him credit for being right until Floyd Aragon and the three with him had returned to town.

He walked toward the hotel. The sun was well down, and its last flaming rays had faded from the scattered clouds. A cricket began to chirp someplace, to be answered by another and by another still.

The saloon adjoining Daybright's store was open and well filled, but the crowd inside was orderly. Dolan climbed the steps to the hotel veranda and went inside. He crossed to the desk, "Luke, put me up a bag of grub. Coffee, sugar, flour, lard, bacon . . . you know what to put into it. I'll pick it up here at the desk half an hour before dawn."

Brodie nodded. Dolan climbed the stairs wearily. He had put in a long day. The county seat was forty-five miles from Pagosa, and a man had to keep moving to make it in a single day.

He went into his room and lighted the lamp. He

removed his boots, pants and shirt. In his underwear, he blew out the lamp and got into bed. He was almost instantly asleep.

✠

Shrill yells in the street awakened him. He lay still a moment, his mind remembering all that had happened yesterday. He knew, then, who was doing the yelling in the street. It was Floyd Aragon and the three who had accompanied him.

Dolan got up. He leaned out the window and stared down into the street. Aragon had pulled his plunging horse to a halt in front of Daybright's saloon, which still had lights in it. The other three also pulled their horses in, dismounted, tied and went inside.

Dolan got back into bed. It was reasonably quiet for a while, but then, as the whisky they were consuming began to be felt by Aragon and the three men with him, they began to yell boisterously. Disgusted, Dolan tried to shut the racket out of his ears, but even when he put the pillow over his head, he still could hear.

Aragon would be drunk and mean and tired tomorrow. He ought to refuse to let the man go, but he knew it wouldn't do any good. If he didn't let Aragon accompany him, he and the others would go on their own. They'd follow, and when the posse closed in on the bank robbers, they'd interfere. No. It would be better if he had them with him and under his control.

He finally fell asleep, and awakened an hour before dawn. He got up, washed, shaved and put on his clothes. He buckled his revolver around his waist.

Brodie wasn't on duty at the desk, but the sack of

grub was waiting there for him. Carrying it and his saddlebags, he headed for the livery.

Several of the posse members were already there—Franks, Grogan and Cal Daybright. Sam Joseph brought Dolan his horse, and he mounted and rode to Ma Ledgerwood's boarding house, after tying the sack of grub on behind along with his blanket roll and saddlebags. There was a rifle in his saddle boot, one of the new repeating Winchesters.

He sat down at the table and waited patiently. There was a somber uneasiness in his thoughts today. Perhaps it was the hour, although it wasn't more than half an hour earlier than his normal rising time. More likely it was the thought of what lay ahead. He supposed he shouldn't have offered Calvin Daybright the chance to go along. He also should flatly refuse to let Aragon go. Both Daybright and Aragon were sure to try to take the law into their own hands if and when the outlaws were caught.

Ma brought the food and Dolan began to eat. The other boarders wished him luck when he left. Most of them worked for the railroad, which was building a line from the county seat westward toward Pagosa and on to the Utah line. The tracks hadn't reached Pagosa yet, but they were only five miles away. The men who boarded at Ma Ledgerwood's rode horseback every day to the end of track.

The ridge east of town was outlined in gray as Dolan pulled his horse to a halt in front of the bank. Daybright, Franks, Grogan, Dunklee and Sam Joseph were already there. Sam had two pack horses. Their panniers were loaded heavily with oats. Dolan looked around for Floyd Aragon, and Jospeh said, 'Him and Cliff Sims are down at the livery saddling up."

"What about the other two?"

Sam Joseph grinned. "I reckon their heads was too big."

Dolan nodded. "Let's go then."

He led out, up Main Street and out of town, letting his horse lope to work out the morning chill. A mile from town he pulled him back to a trot.

Sam Joseph had been studying the road, and Dolan knew that by now Sam had identified the tracks of the horses ridden by the three bank robbers. They might, in places, be obliterated by other tracks, but Sam wasn't going to lose the trail.

Sam's eyes were slightly narrowed and intent. His nostrils were a little flared, as if he was following the trail by smell rather than by sight.

Two miles from town, Dolan heard the pound of hoofs behind. He turned his head and saw Aragon and Sims coming at a run.

Aragon pulled his exicted, already sweating horse to a plunging halt. He said, "No damn use fooling around this close to town. We found where they left the road last night."

Aragon's small eyes were red, both from whisky and from lack of sleep. His mouth was slack.

Dolan said, "We're not fooling around. They're twelve hours ahead of us. Running our horses to where they left the road isn't going to help."

Aragon scowled savagely. "You don't really want to catch them at all, do you? They're twelve hours ahead, and you want to travel at a trot."

Dolan didn't reply. Aragon turned his head and looked at Sims. "How about it, Cliff? Want to go on ahead with me?"

"Sure. Why not?"

Dolan said, "Wait a minute, Floyd. If you're going with this posse, you're going to take orders just like anybody else. Now fall in behind."

Aragon stared at him contemptuously. "I think, by God, you're scared! You've never done nothin' but serve summonses, and you're scared to come up against some real, honest-to-God bad men with guns. Only you've got to make it look like you're trying to catch them, and this is how you do it. Well not me, Sheriff, not me. I'm going to catch them outlaws. I might even string 'em up."

He looked at the other members of the posse one by one. "Who wants to go with me?"

Hack Green looked at Dolan doubtfully. Then he grumbled. "All right. I'll go."

"How about you, Daybright?"

Daybright also looked at Dolan. Dolan met his glance steadily. Daybright shook his head. "I'll stick with the sheriff."

None of the others seemed inclined to go with Aragon. He and Sims and Grogan kicked their horses, pulled around the group and headed up the road.

Dolan kneed his horse close to Franks, his eyes on the rope hanging from Franks's saddle. He said, "Let me have that, Emmett. If I don't stop that big-mouthed fool now, I never will."

Emmett Franks handed him the rope. Dolan raked his horse with his spurs. The startled animal plunged ahead, up the road in pursuit of Floyd Aragon and the other two.

CHAPTER THREE

Dolan HAD SOME second thoughts about what he was doing as he galloped up the road. He knew he was about to earn the everlasting enmity of Floyd Aragon. He also knew if he permitted Aragon and the other two to continue on their own, his control of the posse would be gone.

He spurred his horse, and the animal began to gain on the galloping trio. Aragon, leading, did not look around, probably unaware that anyone was pursuing him. Hack Grogan, a few yards behind Cliff Sims, glanced around, saw the sheriff, and veered aside to let him pass. Once Dolan was past, Hack slowed his horse and in a few moments was far behind.

Sims glanced around as the sheriff's horse came abreast. He yelled, "Floyd! It's Dolan! Look out!"

Dolan kneed his horse sharply against Sims's horse. He felt the contact with a kind of savage pleasure and continued the pressure until Sims's horse was forced off the road. The animal plunged down into the ditch beside the road, nearly falling, nearly unseating Sims as he fought for balance and footing.

Now only Aragon was ahead. He glanced around, saw Dolan and sank his spurs savagely into his horse's sides. Dolan shook out a loop in the rope. He leaned forward over his horse's withers and raked him again with the spurs.

The horse leaped ahead. The distance between Dolan's horse and Aragon's began to close. Less than a dozen yards now separated the two.

Dolan threw the loop. It settled over Aragon's head and shoulders. Dolan let his horse slow slightly and with his hand tightened the loop so that Aragon couldn't throw it off. He didn't want to dump Aragon if he didn't have to. He didn't want to make this any worse than it already was.

Aragon turned his head, his wicked eyes furious. His right hand dropped to his revolver, and he yanked it out, coming around so that he could bring it to bear.

Dolan realized with a shock that Aragon meant to shoot. To free himself he would shoot, probably to kill.

Once he realized that, he didn't hesitate. He drew back on his horse's reins, at the same time dallying the rope around the saddle horn.

Dolan's horse slowed but Aragon's did not. The marshal left the saddle with a savage jerk and hit the road like a sack of oats.

Dolan had been a cowboy once before he became a lawman. He hit the ground almost as soon as Aragon did, and ran along the rope to the downed marshal, who, though stunned, had managed to hold on to his gun.

He kicked the gun out of Aragon's hand. It flew ten feet into the ditch beside the road.

Dolan was angry now. He said furiously, "You damn fool, you'd have shot me, wouldn't you?"

Aragon lay flat on his back, the rope still around his shoulders. The wind had been knocked out of him by the fall, and he was gasping helplessly. But his eyes were virulent.

The rest of the posse members now caught up, including Grogan and Sims. Dolan glanced at them.

"You two have a choice. This is my posse and I'm in charge. If you're not prepared to take orders, then turn around now and get back to town."

Both men looked sullen but both nodded sourly. Dolan heard Aragon stirring and turned to glance at him. Aragon was up on his hands and knees. He was still fighting for breath, but he wasn't gasping so helplessly any more.

Dolan said, "Get up, Floyd, and don't try anything like that again or I'll send you back to town."

Aragon raised his head. His eyes, red from the night before, were narrowed and murderous. He said, "I'll kill you! I'll tear you apart!"

"What about those three bank robbers? A minute ago you couldn't wait to get to the place where they left the road."

"By God, they can wait!" Aragon came up with a rush, charging forward off balance, pumping with his legs to keep himself upright. He struck Dolan with his shoulder in the belly and bowled him back. Dolan fell flat beneath the hoofs of Sam Joseph's horse. The animal reared in fright, then danced nervously away.

Aragon stopped, knocked to his knees by the impact. He now came on again and flung himself at Dolan, who rolled aside.

Dolan was suddenly furious because Aragon had forced him to surrender his dignity in order to enforce his authority. Here he was, rolling in the dirt like a boy in a schoolyard.

He fought to his feet, even as Aragon did likewise half a dozen feet away. Again Aragon charged, blindly, recklessly, like a bull charging a matador.

Dolan stepped aside, and as Aragon came past, he swung a long, looping right that struck Aragon squarely on the ear.

Pain shot clear to Dolan's shoulder, and he cursed himself angrily because he needed his right hand to hold his gun. He couldn't afford to damage it, not for Aragon, not for anyone.

Aragon stumbled and again went to his knees. Dolan supposed it would have been expected of him that he wait until Aragon recovered and got up. But time was short, and he didn't owe the marshal a knock-down-drag-out fight. He didn't owe Aragon anything.

He drew his gun and, stepping close, clipped Aragon with the barrel on the side of the head. Aragon pitched forward, his face burying itself in the dust of the road.

Dolan turned and scowled at the members of the posse. "Load him on his horse, and let's get on with this!"

He walked to the ditch beside the road and picked up the marshal's revolver. He put it into one of his own saddlebags. Then he mounted his horse and coiled the rope. He handed it to Emmett Franks, who was grinning. Franks said, "Whew! I don't think I'll try crossin' you."

Dolan felt some of the anger draining out of him. He managed to erase his frown. "Come on, let's go."

He led out, and the others followed, except for Sims and Grogan, who were trying to boost Aragon, still unconscious, onto his horse. There was no elation in Dolan. He had reestablished his authority, but the cost was too high. Aragon was a formidable adversary. He was mean and savage and violent, and he never forgot anything. He was capable of shooting a man in the back if he couldn't kill him any other way.

He shook his head impatiently. There was no use borrowing trouble. And yet his uneasiness would not go away. In this posse he had Aragon, who was now angry enough to kill him any way he could. He had Cal Daybright, grief-stricken over the death of his little girl, who might try to kill the outlaws when they were caught. He had Miles Dunklee, too soft to keep up but the one who had lost the money and who was therefore entitled to go along. He had Cliff Sims, an ardent admirer of Aragon, who would do anything Aragon told him to. And he had Hack Grogan, another admirer of Aragon, not as dangerous as Sims, but a man to watch anyway.

And as if that wasn't enough potential trouble, there were three smart, desperate outlaws ahead.

✠

The sun came up over the high rims to the east. Several times the road crossed the creek on bridges. Dolan noticed that two of these were beginning to undercut at the ends from the floodwaters. He made a mental note to tell the county commissioners about it when he returned.

Sam Joseph rode in the lead, his eyes constantly studying the ground. At the crest of a rise, Dolan glanced around. About a mile behind he could see the three horses of Aragon, Sims and Grogan coming on abreast. Aragon was now upright in his saddle, although he appeared to be slumped forward. He had probably regained consciousness, Dolan thought. And if he'd thought he had a bad headache earlier this morning, he knew differently now. He'd be no threat today. He was too damn sick to bother anyone.

Three hours after leaving town, Sam Joseph pulled off the road and stopped. "Here's where they left the road."

Dolan nodded, "Stay on their trail. I figure it will wind around in the brush for a while. We'll go on to the foot of the Horse Ridge Trail. If I find their tracks, I'll fire a couple of shots."

Joseph nodded and, without further comment, rode

away into the sagebrush following the outlaws' trail. Dolan led off straight up the ridge.

Ute Plateau covered three thousand square miles and rose above the valleys by twenty-five hundred feet. It was cut in numerous places by various creeks and dry washes and was bordered on the south by Grand River, on the north by White River, on the west by the vast Utah desert.

Below its towering rims, some of which rose a sheer five hundred feet, was a steep, shaly slide on which practically nothing grew, and below that a series of low, sagebrush- and cedar-covered hills.

Dolan knew this route, having been over it before. He took the lead, his horse walking now. The other posse members strung out behind. Miles Dunklee was already beginning to shift uncomfortably in his saddle, and Dolan wondered how long he was going to last.

Daybright's face was grim, but it was patient, too. His eyes sometimes showed pain, but the anger of last night seemed to have gone from him. Dolan watched him covertly, tyring to evaluate him. He wouldn't underestimate Calvin Daybright, he told himself. Once the outlaws were in custody, he'd watch Daybright like a hawk.

Franks, like Sam Joseph, had no personal ax to grind. It was comforting to know that these two, at least, were reliable.

With Dolan leading, the four wound through fragrant sagebrush and cedars for about a mile. At last Dolan reached the foot of the Horse Ridge Trail.

It led straight up a long, sharp-spined ridge, broke left into a ravine, followed that for a couple of miles, then broke out, zigzagged across the shaly slope and at last climbed out through the crumbling sandstone rim at a point where it was no more than thirty or forty feet high.

Dolan studied the rocky ground as he rode. There were tracks here, but until he found soft ground he wouldn't be able to definitely identify them, and he didn't want to make any mistakes.

Half a mile along the ridge, he found a place where the ground was soft and damp and the tracks were plainly identifiable. He stopped, dismounted and turned to the three men with him. "Take your saddles off and cool your horses' backs. We'll be here half an hour waiting for Sam Joseph to catch up." He drew his revolver and fired two shots into the air.

He removed his saddle and laid it on the ground. He sat down, put his back to a twisted cedar and rolled himself a wheat-straw cigarette. He inhaled, watching the trail leading back in the direction from which they had come.

After about twenty minutes, Aragon, Sims and Grogan appeared. Aragon's eyes were narrowed with pain, and there was a knot on one side of his head from which a trickle of blood had run and dried. He glared murderously at Dolan, but when Dolan steadily met his stare, he looked away. Neither Sims nor Grogan would meet the sheriff's eyes.

Another ten minutes passed. At last Sam Joseph came up the trail, his horse walking unhurriedly. Dolan got to his feet. "Saddle up and let's go."

Sam Joseph rode on ahead, following the trial. Aragon and Sims and Grogan, since their horses hadn't been unsaddled, followed him. Dolan and the others saddled and brought up the rear.

In the ravine, Sam Joseph startled a small herd of deer, and they bounded up the steep, shaly slope in great, stiff-legged jumps. At intervals, because the trail was steep, Sam halted his horse to rest. Each time, Dolan could hear Aragon grumbling sourly at the delay.

What he ought to do, he thought, was to let Aragon and Sims and Grogan go on ahead. Let them run their horses to death. That would be one way of getting rid of them. But he knew he couldn't do it. He couldn't take the risk. If they did happen to catch the outlaws, there was a chance they'd kill them, take the money and themselves become fugitives.

Sam Joseph was now less than a hundred yards ahead. Close on his heels rode Aragon, and behind him, Sims and Grogan. Dolan came next, followed by Daybright and Emmett Franks. Miles Dunklee brought up the rear, already lagging almost a quarter mile.

The column came out of the ravine and took the narrow, zigzag trail across the slide. The leaders kicked rocks loose, and they tumbled down, striking those following. But they were small rocks that did little more than sting.

Sam Joseph reached the narrow trail cut out of the crumbling sandstone rim. He took this trail alone, and the others waited until he was out on top. One at a time, then, they followed, until at last the entire posse was above the rim.

Here, there were tall spruce and pine, and the ground underfoot was soft with a century's accumulation of needles, rotting in the shade. Frowning slightly, Sam Joseph rode up through the timber, leaning far to one side in order to better see the ground. At the crest, where the timber petered out into sagebrush again, he straightened and flashed Dolan a smile. He had the trail again, and now he kicked his horse into a steady, mile-eating trot. Dolan pushed ahead, past Sims and Grogan and Aragon, until he was riding less than a dozen yards in back of Sam. Aragon's eyes on his back gave him a feeling of uneasiness that was almost physical, but he didn't turn his head.

CHAPTER FOUR

THE TRAIL CLIMBED through the sagebrush to the crest of the ridge, and here, on the spine of the highest point of land for miles, Dolan could see the deep gash in the plateau that was Poison Creek on his right, and the equally rugged gash on his left that marked the course of Colorow Creek.

To right and left, on the slopes dropping away toward both drainages, were thick groves of aspen trees, some of whose trunks were a foot thick or more.

The land ahead was not as flat as it had first appeared from below. It consisted of rolling ridges and shallow valleys, in which the serviceberry brush and oak brush was occasionally so thick a horse could scarcely penetrate it, so high a rider couldn't see over it.

Dust rose from the horses' hoofs. The sun climbed steadily across the sky until it reached its zenith overhead.

At noon, Dolan called to Sam Joseph to halt, and they stopped at a small trickle of water and let the horses drink. The men dismounted and walked back and forth to loosen muscles turned stiff by the long morning's ride.

Dolan hadn't seen Miles Dunklee for a couple of hours and knew he must be a long ways behind. A

26

trot is hard on a man unused to riding, but it is an easy gait for a horse to maintain and one that eats the miles.

Aragon dismounted and laid down in the shade of a tall clump of sagebrush. His face was gray with pain. He kept his eyes narrowed against the glare of the sun overhead. Dolan stared at him without pity. He wished there was some way of getting rid of Aragon, but he couldn't think of what it would be.

They had been resting half an hour when Miles Dunklee rode into sight. He slid from his horse and collapsed weakly on the ground. Dolan looked down at him, compassion in his face. "Miles, why don't you go back? I'll recover the money and return it to the bank."

Dunklee shook his head. "I'll make it."

Dolan shrugged. He knew Dunklee wouldn't make it. The next couple of days would be torture for the banker, and for nothing, because in the end he would have to go back anyway. But there was no use arguing.

Some of the men ate. Others did not. Dolan made no attempt to dictate to them. He'd told them all to bring enough food for a week. If they ran out before the week was up, they'd have to go hungry and they'd get no sympathy from him.

After an hour's rest, he saddled up his horse. Sam Joseph, Franks and Daybright followed suit without being told. Aragon remained lying in the shade. His two side-kicks, Grogan and Sims, stayed with him. Dunklee groaned and tried to get up, but fell weakly back.

Again Sam Joseph led out. In midafternoon, they crossed the head of the Colorow Creek drainage, heading west, and now, in this highest part of the Ute Plateau, it was rolling, timbered prairie land, with no deep canyons in sight.

An hour after crossing the head of Colorow Creek, Sam Joseph pulled his horse to a sudden halt. Dolan, a dozen yards behind, pulled up beside him. Sam pointed to horse tracks crossing the trail they had been following. He said in his deep voice, "Unshod Indian ponies, Sheriff. I make it mebee six."

Dolan waited. The tracker rode back along the trail made by the Indian ponies for a hundred yards, studying the ground carefully. He returned to the sheriff. He confirmed his own estimate. "Six. Likely a huntin' party off the reservation. Two of the ponies are heavily loaded, so they likely packing a couple of deer. They crossed the trail we followed this morning. They stopped and took a look at it and went on, but that don't mean they forgot it. It could mean they just want us to think they forgot it."

Dolan continued to wait. Sam Joseph grinned faintly at him. "I'd like to track them Injuns for a mile or two. Why don't you stay on this trail? I'll catch you by an' by."

Dolan nodded agreement. Sam Joseph rode away, following the trail of the renegade Utes, and Dolan led Franks and Daybright along the outlaws' trail. The sun slid slowly down the western sky. A couple of hours before sundown, he heard horses coming on behind. He turned his head and saw Aragon, Sims and Grogan, loping their horses in order to catch up.

Not long afterward, Sam Joseph rode in from the side. He pulled up beside Dolan. "I guessed right. They turn west half a mile past where they crossed the outlaws' trail. They still four hours ahead of us."

Dolan frowned. The six Indians could complicate things, particularly if they happened to catch the fugitives before the posse did. But there was nothing he could do about it. They would have to halt soon for the night. It might be a couple of days before they caught up, with either the Indians or the fugitives.

The trail led down a long ravine, and they entered a scattering of tall, red-trunked pines and, a few moments afterward, glimpsed a log cabin through the screen of trees. Seconds later a rifle boomed, and a bullet tore bark from a tree trunk half a dozen feet from Sam Joseph's head.

The tracker was instantly off his horse and behind the tree, his rifle in his hands. Dolan abandoned his own horse with equal haste and took cover behind another tree. Franks and Daybright followed suit.

Fifty yards back, hidden in the trees, Aragon and the two with him halted their horses and sat waiting None of the three showed any inclination to come forward.

Dolan frowned with puzzlement. He couldn't believe the outlaws would have been foolish enough to stop. They must know a posse was on their trail. And even if one of their number was wounded . . .

He said, "I'll bet it's the one that Dunklee shot. They must have left him here."

He turned his head and called softly, "Franks, you and Daybright stay where you are. Put a bullet into the cabin often enough to keep his head down while Sam and I circle and get behind the place."

He didn't wait for the pair to acknowledge his order but moved out immediately, keeping himself concealed by brush and trees, making a wide circle so that he would not be seen. The Negro moved off in the opposite direction, disappearing immediately from Dolan's view.

The land dropped away sharply now. Through the timber Dolan could see a yawning canyon, its rim less than three hundred yards below the cabin, which had been built here originally, he supposed, because of the abundant spring water welling out of the ground. Faintly he could hear the small stream tumbling down toward the waterfall that pitched off the perpendicular sandstone rim.

Again he caught a glimpse of the cabin through the trees and now angled toward it, running in a half crouch, rifle in hand, alert eyes on the cabin window ahead of him. He reached the log wall without being fired upon and put his back to it, breathing hard and fast.

When he was again breathing normally, he transferred his rifle to his left hand and drew his revolver with his right. He thumbed the hammer back, crept to the window, crouched to get under it, then raised up quickly, the revolver held slightly higher than his head.

He saw a shadowy figure inside the place, silhouetted against the light coming from the front window. Quickly he smashed the window glass with the revolver barrel, at the same time pointing his gun at the figure inside the place. "Don't turn around or you're dead!"

The figure froze, half-turned toward him. At that instant Sam Joseph smashed the window on the opposite side of the room and issued his own sharp warning not to turn.

The rifle held by the cabin's occupant clattered to the floor. Dolan said, "Stay put, Sam. I'll go to the door."

He circled the cabin at a run and burst in through the unlocked front door. He stopped, staring with disbelief. The figure facing him was not one of the bank robbers. It was a woman, with tears welling from her eyes and spilling across her cheeks. Dolan said, "Well for God's sake . . . !"

Her tears now came in a flood. Dolan said helplessly, "Ma'am, we're not going to hurt you. I'm Sheriff Dolan and these men are members of my posse."

The woman collapsed into a chair and bent forward burying her face in her hands. Dolan said, "Ma'am, it's all right," and when that didn't help, he asked, "Did those three hurt you when they were here this morning?"

She raised her head. She stared across the room toward the bed, and suddenly Dolan understood. A man lay there, his hands folded on his chest. His eyes were closed, his face like wax. Dolan said, "Your husband, ma'am?"

She nodded, glancing at him directly for the first time. She was, he supposed, about thirty. Her hair was a dark rich brown, put up in a bun straying in wisps across her face. She was a pretty woman, even with her eyes red and her face streaked with tears. He asked, "What happened?"

It was a moment before she spoke. Somehow he had known what her voice would be like, but it was a pleasant surprise anyway. She said, "They demanded fresh horses and my husband refused. He tried to reach his gun and they shot him. They took our horses and turned their own horses loose."

Dolan thought of the Indians. It was possible the Utes had missed this cabin, but he didn't believe they had. Nor did he believe the Utes would have continued to follow the outlaws' trail after they had spotted this lone woman here. They had probably only been waiting until dark.

He crossed to the door and went outside. He waved the rest of the posse in. When Daybright and Franks, Aragon and the other two arrived, he said, "Floyd, you supervise those two with you in the digging of a grave. There's a man dead in here."

He turned his head when he saw Aragon staring. The woman was standing in the door. He asked, "Where would you like to have him buried, ma'am?"

She shrugged wearily. "I don't suppose it matters much."

Dolan pointed to the hillside. "Up there, Aragon. There's a lean-to at the back of the cabin. I expect the shovels are in there."

Aragon continued to stare at the woman, but without turning his head he spoke harshly to Sims and Grogan. "Get the shovels and get at it."

Dolan turned his head. "What's your name, ma'am?"

"Flora. Flora Doniphan."

He said, "We'll stay here tonight and bury your husband, but tomorrow you'll have to come with us. We spotted the trail of half a dozen Ute renegades back there a ways."

She stared at him confusedly. "I have no place to go."

"Don't you have any family?"

She shook her head, then glanced into the house. "Only him."

"Have you been married long?"

"A year."

"And before that?"

She hesitated, flushing painfully. If she had confessed, it could not have been more plain. She had been a saloon girl before her marriage to Doniphan.

Dolan said, "You'll have to come, ma'am. It's not safe for you to stay here now."

She nodded. "There's nothing to keep me here."

Dolan turned his head. Aragon's eyes still rested on Flora Doniphan. Dolan said sharply, "Floyd, get up there and show them where to put that gravel!"

Aragon stared at Dolan balefully for a long moment. Then without a word he trudged up the slope to where Sims and Grogan waited, leaning on the shovels they had found in the lean-to shed.

Dolan turned to Sam Joseph. "Think you could catch the outlaws' horses, Sam? Mrs. Doniphan will need one of them to ride."

Sam Joseph nodded silently. He mounted and rode away, making a big circle of the cabin in order to pick up the trail. Dolan said, "Get your things together, ma'am. We'll be leaving here at dawn."

She nodded silently and disappeared into the cabin. Mike Dunklee came riding down the ravine. He slid off his horse and almost fell. He limped to the stream, knelt and splashed water onto his face.

Dolan frowned. Flora Doniphan was sure to complicate an already difficult task. He had not missed the way Floyd Aragon had looked at her. But he didn't dare let her remain. Not with that band of renegades running loose.

CHAPTER FIVE

Dolan went out and unsaddled his horse. He rubbed the animal down, watered him, then picketed him to graze. He returned to the cabin.

Aragon, who had started down off the hillside, went back to the grave, scowling, when he saw Dolan go inside. Dolan grinned faintly to himself.

He knew it would be awkward for everyone to eat supper with a dead man in the room. He said, "If you have a blanket, ma'am, I can wrap your husband in it and carry him outside."

"Any of those will do. I won't be coming back."

"Isn't this a homestead, ma'am? Don't you have cattle and horses here?"

She nodded. "Yes. But perhaps I can find someone who will buy them from me."

"I'll talk to Emmett Franks. He has a ranch at the head of Poison Creek. And he's an honest man."

"Thank you, Sheriff."

He crossed the room and wrapped the body in two blankets. It was with some difficulty that he lifted it and carried it outside. He carried it to the foot of the hillside below the grave and laid it down.

He returned to the cabin. Flora Doniphan's face was paler than before, but otherwise she seemed the same. She was busy cooking supper and setting the long, rough-hewn table. "How many will there be?"

"With yourself, ma'am, nine."

She turned her head, a faint smile touching her lips. "Couldn't you call me something besides ma'am? Flora or Mrs. Doniphan? Anything seems better than ma'am."

"Sure. I'll call you Mrs. Doniphan." He didn't want to start anything that might lead to easy familiarity, like calling her by her given name. Aragon already had ideas about Flora Doniphan.

He went outside again and washed in the narrow stream. Aragon and Sims and Grogan came down off the slope. Sam Joseph returned, driving the three horses that had belonged to the outlaws. He herded them into the pole corral. Dolan noticed that one of them had blood on his flank, but there was no wound to account for it. It must be the wounded outlaw's blood, he thought.

Flora Doniphan came to the door and called. The men filed inside. Dunklee sat down gingerly on the long bench. He looked pale and sick. Dolan doubted if he'd be able to travel tomorrow. He wondered how safe it would be for Dunklee to remain here with the six Utes still skulking around.

Flora passed the food, and the men began to eat hungrily. She did not sit down, and when Dolan mentioned it, she said, "I can't eat, Sheriff, but I'll be all right."

Outside, light faded from the sky. It turned gray and gradually deepened into black. Flora lighted two lamps and put them on the table. Dolan finished eating and rolled himself a wheat-straw cigarette. The others lighted up their cigars and pipes.

Sam Joseph helped Flora Doniphan pick up the table, and after that he washed the dishes for her. Then he went out, picked up her husband's body and carried it up the hill to the waiting grave. Dolan carried one lamp, and Emmett Franks another. Flora brought a worn-looking Bible, and while Dolan held the lamp, she read from it.

With ropes, Dolan, Franks, Daybright and Grogan lowered the body into the grave. Flora sprinkled a handful of earth into it, then turned and hurried down the hill to the cabin. She disappeared inside.

Dolan and Franks filled the grave. Carrying the lamps, they walked back down the hill. Dolan knocked on the door, and when Flora came, gave her the lamps. Turning, he called, "You'd all better get some sleep. We'll be leaving as soon as it's light enough to trail."

He spread his blankets at the edge of the clearing. He wanted to be able to see the cabin door. He didn't think Aragon would try anything tonight, but he didn't want to take the chance. He'd busted Aragon early this morning successfully, but if he locked horns with the man again, somebody was likely to end up dead.

The lamps went out in the cabin. The small stream made its rushing sound as it tumbled along toward the canyon rim. Wind sighed through the pines, and somewhere nearby a pack of coyotes quarreled on a hill. Dolan listened carefully for several moments and decided they were really coyotes and not Indians.

There was little danger, he decided, from the Utes. They might be off the reservation hunting, but they weren't looking for a pitched battle with a posse that outnumbered them. They might have molested Flora had she been alone in the cabin tonight. They might conceivably kill Dunklee if he remained behind, just for the sport of it. But they weren't going to take risks they didn't have to take.

Dolan slept, but lightly, waking often at some small noise. Nobody came near the cabin, and Dolan sup-

posed Aragon was still too sick to be interested in
Flora Doniphan. He awoke half an hour before dawn
and roused the men. Shortly thereafter he saw lamp-
light inside the house and smoke issuing from the
chimney.

Before it was fully light, Flora came to the door
and called the men to eat. Half an hour later, she
pulled the door closed behind her for the last time
and allowed Dolan to help her mount. Behind her
sidesaddle was a bulging carpetbag containing everything she meant to take with her.

Surprisingly, Miles Dunklee had managed to saddle
and mount. Sam Joseph led off, following the trail as
it skirted the precipitous rim and continued west. Undoubtedly, Dolan thought, the outlaws had trailed
Doniphan down here from the top of the ridge,
hoping to find fresh horses. They'd found them, all
right, and could have paid for them with the money
they had stolen from the bank. Instead they had tried
to take the horses by force and had killed Doniphan
when he tried to prevent the theft.

Dolan's jaw hardened as he stared at Flora riding
ahead of him. She was a widow and alone because the
three outlaws preferred to steal horses rather than
pay for them. Killing Susan Daybright might have
been an accident and unavoidable. Killing Doniphan
had been murder, senseless and unnecessary.

He let his horse lag slightly until he was riding
abreast of Emmett Franks. "She says her husband had
cattle and horses. I told her I'd ask if you'd be interested in buying them."

Franks nodded without hesitation. "I'll gather
them up and drive them to Pagosa and sell them for
her. Just as soon as we get back."

"I'll tell her." Dolan hesitated a moment more.
"You know this country a lot better than I do. How

many places are there ahead of us where they can get fresh horses?"

Franks frowned faintly. "Nothin' for about thirty miles. Then there's J Diamond. A hundred or so miles beyond that is McGuffy's Trading Post."

"What if they turn north or south?"

"There's nothin' north. The Utah desert is west, and there's nothin' down there this time of year. Not until you reach Salt Lake."

Dolan said, "Let's hope we catch them before they get that far."

They rode in silence for a long time. The trail wound through the tall spruce and yellow pines that fringed the rim, then crossed a stretch of precipitous, shaly slide that terminated, fifty feet below, in a sheer drop-off of several hundred feet.

Sam Joseph was still in the lead, with Flora Doniphan following. Dolan came behind Flora. Earlier, Cal Daybright had been immediately behind him, but now a sudden feeling of uneasiness he could neither explain nor understand made him glance around.

Daybright was no longer immediately behind. Floyd Aragon had taken his place. And Floyd seemed to be having trouble with his horse. The animal kept trying to rear, despite the narrowness of the trail and kept glancing up toward the timber, rolling his eyes and laying back his ears. Aragon cursed him sourly, then glanced at Dolan apologetically. "He must smell a bear."

Dolan said, "Funny none of the other horses do." Aragon's horse puzzled him, but Aragon puzzled him even more. All day yesterday Aragon had glared murderously at him. Now, suddenly, he was being civil, and that couldn't help rousing Dolan's suspicions.

He glanced left toward the precipice. If a horse lost his footing here, both horse and man would slide and roll to the rim, then tumble over to fall several hundred feet to the rocks below. It could happen so quickly, no one could ever be sure how it had happened or why. Certainly nothing could be proved.

A cold chill ran along Dolan's spine because he suddenly understood why Aragon's horse was acting up. Aragon was forcing it by alternately spurring and yanking on the reins. At any moment the confused horse could get out of control and plunge ahead. He would crowd past the sheriff's horse on the upper side of the trail. Dolan's horse, having been forced to lose both footing and balance, would slide and roll to the rim and go over helplessly. Even if Dolan abandoned the saddle, he would probably follow the horse over the rim. The slope below the trail was almost forty-five degrees. There was nothing to cling to, and the shaly rock surface had a tendency to slide.

The trail angled upward and entered timber less than three hundred yards ahead. Aragon would have to make his move immediately if it was to succeed.

Dolan glanced around again. There was a small smile on Aragon's thin-lipped mouth. And suddenly his nervously fidgeting horse lunged forward, angling toward the upper half of the trail. If the horse succeeded in getting his head past the rump of Dolan's horse, Aragon's deadly maneuver was certain to succeed.

Dolan spurred his own horse instantly, and the startled animal leaped ahead. At the same time, Dolan reined him toward the right so that he climbed the slope slightly above the trail. The footing here was just as treacherous as below the trail, but the trail itself would give the horse a chance to regain his footing if he began to slip.

Dolan turned his head. He yanked his gun and swinging around in the saddle, leveled it at Aragon. He said, "If you don't get control of that horse and drop back, I'm going to kill you."

Aragon opened his mouth to protest; he closed it without saying anything. He drew in on his horse's reins, and the animal slowed immediately. Dolan dropped back, and Aragon growled, "What the hell's eatin' you?"

Dolan said, "Nothing now," and shoved his gun back into its holster again. Ahead, Sam Joseph disappeared into the timber, with Flora following. Dolan released a long sigh as his horse entered the timber immediately behind.

He was going to have to watch Aragon every minute, he told himself. The man would kill without hesitation if he got the chance.

Once more, now, the trail ascended to the spine of the plateau. Dolan called to Sam Joseph, "See any more of those Ute pony tracks?"

Waiting for the Negro tracker to answer, he grinned shakily to himself. Probably only he and Aragon knew how close he had come to death a few moments before. He doubted if those behind Aragon, watching, had even realized what was going on.

A new respect for his adversary was born in him. He knew now that if Aragon succeeded in killing him it would be in such a way that nobody would realize or be able to prove what he had done.

In answer to his question, Sam Joseph turned in his saddle and shook his head. "They stayed back there at the cabin, Mr. Dolan. I figure they was after Mrs. Doniphan."

"What do you think they'll do when they find out she came with us?"

"Why, they goin' to follow us, Mr. Dolan. They ain't got nothin' better to do with their time. They got a couple of deer, so they ain't worried about what they're goin' to eat. They off the reservation an' lookin' for trouble an' excitement. But they won't jump us 'less they figure they got a good chance to win."

Dolan nodded. From here he could see about half a mile back along the trail. He couldn't see Miles Dunklee, though, and he frowned worriedly. Perhaps he could leave Dunklee at J Diamond, thirty miles ahead, he thought. If the renegade Utes didn't get him first.

Westward, ever westward went the trail. Even where it crossed rocky, shale ground, Sam Joseph never hesitated or went astray He was almost like a hound, thought Dolan, trailing by smell instead of sight. If he caught the outlaws, it would be largely because Sam Joseph was along.

They should reach J Diamond Ranch tonight, he thought, and settled himself more comfortably in his saddle. Flora Doniphan, riding ahead of him, held his interest and his glance.

Dolan had been married once, fifteen years ago. His wife had lived a year, and he had been alone ever since.

There were advantages to living alone, he thought now. Particularly for a sheriff, who was away from home a good bit of the time. But there were times, like now, when the sight of a pretty woman made him realize how empty his life actually was. Flora Doniphan was indeed a pretty woman. He watched her, watched the graceful way she rode, watched the way her hand sometimes came up to brush a wisp of hair away from her face.

CHAPTER SIX

IN MIDMORNING DOLAN halted suddenly. He held up a hand, halting those behind. To Sam Joseph, riding a dozen yards ahead, he called, "Sam. Listen."

Sam Joseph stopped his horse. There was still some noise, that of a rattled bit as a horse tossed his head to shake off a fly, the swishing of the horses' tails, an occasional scraping of a hoof against the rocky ground as one of the horses fidgeted or shifted his feet. But even above these sounds Dolan heard what had halted him. Shots, faint and far away, back along the trail over which they just had come.

He said, "It's Dunklee. Those damn Utes are after him." He supposed Dunklee must be at least half a mile behind. Sounds carried well in this high, clear air. He said, "Franks. Daybright. Come with me."

He whirled his horse and spurred in the direction from which they had just come. He stopped beside Aragon long enough to return the marshal's gun. Having done that, he yelled, "Keep going, Sam. We'll catch up with you."

He rode away, and the posse was lost to sight, except for Franks and Daybright, following. Dolan hated to run the horses, but he didn't want to arrive too late and find Dunklee already dead.

The shots continued sporadically. Dolan guessed

that the guns the Utes had were Springfield .45-70s or something similar. They had a deep, booming sound that indicated a large caliber. Each of Dunklee's shots, on the other hand, was distinguishable by its sharp, distinctive crack. Dolan grinned faintly to himself. Dunklee might be saddlesore, but that didn't prevent him from firing his gun. He remembered that it was Dunklee who had run out of the bank and shot one of the fleeing outlaws while everybody else in town was still trying to figure out what was happening.

As it turned out, the distance Dunklee had lagged behind was almost exactly three quarters of a mile. To Dolan, it seemed like much more than that. He kept wishing he had refused Dunklee permission to come along. He'd known the banker couldn't keep up, that he couldn't stand the pace. Dunklee probably hadn't sat a saddle for a dozen years. Dolan would have bet his thighs and buttocks were raw. The miracle was that he kept up this well.

Sam Joseph had counted the tracks of six horses, which meant the Utes outnumbered the four of them. Short of the scene of the attack by three hundred yards and screened by aspen trees, Dolan raised a hand and pulled his plunging horse to a sudden halt. The animal was sweating heavily and breathing hard. Dolan cursed softly beneath his breath. A lot was going to be demanded of these three horses in the next few days, and he hated to wear them out like this.

He said, "Dunklee is still alive and is probably holed up in some rocks or heavy brush, so there's no hurry and no use going off half cocked. You two stay here while I make a circle and see where Dunklee is and where the Indians are."

Franks and Daybright nodded. Dolan swung from his horse and handed the reins to Franks, who had also dismounted. Franks was the steady one of the two. Daybright's eyes were excited and his hands were trembling. Dolan supposed that this was the first time in Daybright's life that he had faced the prospect of shooting at another man, or getting shot at himself. It wasn't surprising that he was nervous and afraid. Dolan grinned reassuringly at him as he moved away from the aspens and heavy service-berry brush.

He was closer to the shooting now. He peered cautiously through the brush.

Dunklee had found shelter in the center of some upthrusting rock outcroppings. Dolan heard one of the Indians' bullets strike a rock and ricochet away, whining, into empty space. A shower of rock dust showed where the bullet had struck.

Now Dunklee raised his head from behind a rock and quickly triggered a shot at the cloud of bluish powder smoke that had billowed from the Indian's gun. Dolan continued to watch until he had placed the positions of all six Indians in his mind. Then, cautiously, he withdrew.

Since there was a rising slope behind Dunklee, the Indians apparently weren't worried that he would escape that way. If he tried, they knew they would see him plainly and be able to bring him down. They had, therefore, not bothered to completely surround the man. They were all on one side of him.

Dolan reached the place he had left Daybright and Franks. He said, "I've got their positions spotted. Tie the horses. We'll work around on foot until we're in back of them, but we'll stay between them and our horses so that they can't break back this way."

Franks and Daybright tied the horses. Dolan led off, circling slightly toward the left in order to get behind the Indians.

After going almost two hundred yards, he stopped. He beckoned Franks, and the old rancher followed him until they both could see through the screen of trees and brush. Dolan whispered, "Find yourself a place. You'll be able to spot the Utes when they shoot. Dunklee is over there in that pile of rocks."

Franks nodded silently, a slight grin on his mouth. Dolan said, "It'll be up to you to see that they don't break past you toward the place we left the horses."

Franks nodded. "Don't worry. They won't get by me."

Dolan withdrew to where he had left Daybright. He moved on ahead, with Daybright following, for another fifty yards. Then he led Daybright through the brush, which was thinner here, necessitating a hands-and-knees approach for the last fifty feet.

Bellied down behind a clump of sagebrush, he pointed out to Daybright the approximate positions of the Utes. "Keep watching for the smoke from their guns. You'll spot their exact positions that way. Don't do any shooting until I do."

Daybright nodded. Dolan could see the knotted muscles standing out along his jaw and understood how much tension there was in him. He gripped Daybright's shoulder and then withdrew cautiously. He continued on for fifty yards, screened by brush, then crawled to the right until he had a good view once more.

From here, he could plainly see two of the Utes, bellied down behind some brush. Two hundred yards farther, he could see a couple of their horses through the trees. He could easily kill the two Utes from here. But he didn't want to kill. He didn't want a big stink with the Indian Bureau if it could be helped.

From a prone position, he took careful aim. What he wanted most of all was to scare the Indians. He drew a bead on the ground slightly to one side of the Indian's face.

He squeezed the trigger carefully. If he pulled the shot, he'd put a bullet into the Indian's head. The rifle roared, and blue powder smoke drolled out in front of him. He saw a geyser of dirt shoot three feet into the air, and he grinned as the Indian leaped to his feet, clawing at his eyes trying to get the dirt out, then charged blindly away through the brush.

Dolan already had a bead on the ground beside the second Indian's head. Daybright was shooting his rifle excitedly at the running Indian, who was visible to him. Franks still hadn't fired his.

Dolan squeezed the trigger again. Again the geyser of dirt shot into the air. The second Indian rolled away from it, knuckling his eyes, which were also full of dirt. Dolan put another shot close to him, forcing him to leap to his feet and run, as the first had done.

Again Daybright fired blindly, missing with every shot, having reloaded his rifle hastily. The other four Utes began to return Daybright's fire, and now Franks began firing, slowly and deliberately. Dolan wished he had warned both men not to try hitting the Indians. But he hadn't and now it was too late.

Dunklee had raised up behind his rock and was also firing. Dolan saw one of the Indians struck and saw him fall. He cursed softly, but the remaining three got up and ran a zigzag course through the scattered brush toward where their horses had been tied.

He yelled, "Hold your fire! That's enough!"

The three reached the horses, which the two with dirt in their eyes apparently had already reached. Dolan heard the rapid drum of hoofs as the five Utes raced away.

He raised up on his hands and knees. The Indian who had been shot was invisible to him. It was probable that the man was only wounded and therefore exceedingly dangerous. He shouted, "Stay right where you are, all of you. I'll see if the one Dunklee shot is still alive."

Cautiously and deliberately, he crawled through

the brush toward the place he had seen the Indian fall. He held his rifle in his left hand, his revolver in his right. He used his elbows to crawl upon.

The sun beat hotly down. Dolan was soaked with sweat. It ran down his forehead and into his eyes, making them smart, making him blink irritably. That damn Indian could have been just stunned. He could be stalking Dolan just as Dolan was stalking him.

Time dragged interminably. But suddenly, immediately ahead of him, there was a crashing of brush and a flash of movement. The next instant, the Ute leaped, and Dolan had only time to roll onto his side and throw up the rifle as a shield.

The Indian had a knife in one hand, his rifle in the other. The rifle must be empty or he would have used it instead of the knife, whose blade now buried itself in the ground inches from Dolan's chest.

Dolan slammed the revolver against the Indian, aiming for his head, already bleeding profusely from a deep scalp wound, but hitting the man's naked shoulder instead. The Ute yanked his knife from the ground and poised to stab with it again.

Dolan fired, almost directly into the Indian's face, throwing himself aside simultaneously. He expected to see the Ute driven back by the force of the bullet. Instead the Indian seem blinded by grains of burning powder and by smoke. He slashed with the knife instead of stabbing with it, and Dolan felt the burn of it rake across his chest, cutting through vest and shirt, cutting skin and flesh beneath.

And suddenly triggered by the burning pain, all the worries and frustrations of this posse became intolerable. Ragging, he struggled to his knees and on up to his feet. He thumbed back the hammer of his revolver and brought the gun to bear.

But he couldn't shoot, because he realized the Indian couldn't see. The man was staring around with streaming, reddened eyes, poised to stab with the knife, whose blade was red with Dolan's blood, but unable to see his enemy.

Stepping back, Dolan uttered a dusgusted curse. He said, "Get out of here, and be damned glad I don't kill you where you stand. You and your pals had better get back to the reservation and quit trailing us because next time it ain't going to be so easy for you. Understand?"

The Ute did not reply. He was a young brave, perhaps twenty-five, strongly muscled and deep-chested, though squat and bowlegged, as were most of the Utes. But he understood all right. He turned, apparently now able to see a little out of his streaming eyes, and headed for the place the six had tied their horses earlier.

Franks, Daybright and Dunklee now approached. Dunklee asked unbelievingly, "You're not going to let him go, are you? He tried to kill me, and he did his best to kill you just now!"

Dolan asked, "Have you any idea how much commotion killing a reservation Indian can cause? I could be filling out forms for weeks. There could be half a dozen investigators from the Indian Bureau pestering me. They might even bring murder charges against me and try me in federal court. Huh uh. I'd rather let him go."

The Ute found his horse, mounted and rode away, following the other five. Dolan looked at Dunklee. "Can you ride?"

Dunklee nodded. "I guess so but no faster than a walk."

"That isn't fast enough. And I don't dare let you lag behind again."

Dunklee said doubtfully, "I can try keeping up."

Dolan stared at him irritably. "I warned you, Mr. Dunklee, that you'd have to keep up no matter what.

I can't lose any more time with you or we'll never catch those three and get your money back. Now make up your mind. Can you keep up or can't you? If you can't, I'll just have to lash you on your horse belly down until we get someplace where you'll be safe."

Dunklee's face flushed. "I'll keep up, Sheriff. Don't you worry about me."

Dolan nodded shortly. "Get your horse and get going, then. I'll stay behind just to make sure you don't fall behind."

Dunklee's lips were compressed with anger. He limped toward the rocks where his horse was tied. A few moments later he came riding out, anger still showing in his face.

Dolan stared at him with satisfaction. If he could keep Dunklee mad enough, the man might manage to keep up, a least until they stopped for the night, at which time he could construct a travois for the banker to ride as far as J Diamond Ranch.

He could now feel the wetness of blood from the knife slash across his chest. It would be painful, but it wasn't deep and would stop bleeding soon. Fortunately he had another shirt in his saddlebags.

CHAPTER SEVEN

DOLAN HAD EXPECTED it to take until midafternoon to overtake Sam Joseph and the others, but it was only a little after noon when he saw Sam Joseph ahead, riding at a walk, leading the two pack animals.

Franks, Daybright and Dunklee were immediately ahead. Dunklee kept shifting in his saddle, his face white and drawn with pain. Dolan galloped around the three and overtook Sam Joseph, who halted his horse and turned, glowering.

Dolan had never seen Sam Joseph so thoroughly furious before. The Negro's eyes were narrowed. His mouth was tight. Muscles played along his jaws.

Dolan hauled his horse to a halt. He asked, "Where's Aragon?"

Sam Joseph gestured shortly with his head. "He went on. I couldn't stop him. He just went on."

"What the hell do you mean, he just went on? You're the tracker. He was supposed to stay behind you."

"Well he didn't, Mr. Dolan. He . . ." Sam Joseph stared down at his hands, big, calloused and very black. They were trembling. He said, "Mr. Dolan, I ain't never been so mad in my whole damn life. That marshal, he ordered me to gallop. He said we was wastin' time. He said we wasn't never goin' to catch them outlaws less'n we went faster. I said I wasn't goin' to try followin' that trail at a gallop. I said you was back there and if we went at a gallop you wasn't never goin' to be able to catch up to us. He said that was fine, that he could do a better job of catchin' them outlaws than you could anyhow."

For several moments Sam Joseph stared at his trembling hands where they rested, clasped, on his saddle horn. "Mr. Dolan, he insulted me. He called me a name. I purty near pulled my gun on him, Mr. Dolan, but I didn't. I gritted my teeth and I clenched my fists and I kept my hand off my gun. He grabbed the reins of Mrs. Doniphan's horse and rode off at a gallop. Them other two, Hack Grogan an' Cliff Sims, they followed him. I thought about goin' after them to see they didn't hurt Mrs. Doniphan, but I figured they'd only ride that much faster if I did. So I just held my horse to a walk waitin' for you to catch up to me."

Franks, Daybright and Dunklee had now caught up. Dolan glanced at them. "Aragon's taken Mrs. Doniphan and Sims and Grogan and gone on ahead, at a gallop, Sam Joseph says." He looked at Emmett Franks. "Emmett, how far is J Diamond now?"

Franks frowned, staring ahead along the trail. He said "Twenty-five miles. We'll have to go some to reach it before dark."

Dolan said, "Aragon will get there a long time before that. He'll probably reach it about the middle of the afternoon."

Franks nodded. "If he left when we heard those shots and turned back and if he travels at a gallop most of the way, he'll be there a couple or three hours from now."

"And that'll give him five hours of daylight afterward. How many horses do they usually keep around

J Diamond, do you know? And who owns it, any-way?"

"It belonds to a man named Jack Diamond. That's where the brand comes from. He ain't usually got more'n two or three horses in his corral, unless he's breakin' broncs."

"Does he break broncs this time of year?"

Franks nodded. "This is the time of year he's usually breakin' 'em."

"Then he could have several half-broke horses besides the two or three?"

"He could."

Dolan muttered a disgusted curse.

Daybright asked, "Why do you suppose they took Mrs. Doniphan? She'll only slow them down."

Dolan turned his head. "Why do you think, Mr. Daybright? She's a handsome woman, and Aragon hasn't been able to keep his hungry eyes off her."

He shrugged wearily. "All right. Dismount. Unsad-dle and rub your horses down. We'll give 'em half an hour's rest, and while we're doing that, we'll build a travois for Mr. Dunklee to ride."

Daybright asked, "Isn't that foolish? Shouldn't we be moving on as fast as we possibly can?"

"Half an hour's rest will do the horses good, and they'll travel better for it." He swung from his horse and unsaddled him. He rubbed him down vigorously with the saddle blanket. working up a considerable sweat doing it. The others were slower, but they fol-lowed suit. When Dolan had finished rubbing down his horse, he stood back and fanned him for several minutes with the saddle blanket to cool him off.

Turning, he said, "I don't suppose anybody's got a hatchet for cutting wood."

Sam Joseph said, "I got one, Mr. Dolan."

"Then go cut a couple of stout travois poles. Emmett, I'll need your rope. The county will buy you another one."

Franks took down his rope. It was stiff and hard, difficult stuff with which to tie knots that would hold, but it was all there was.

The sounds of chopping came from a nearby grove of aspen trees. After ten minutes, Sam Joseph returned with two neatly trimmed travois poles. Dolan took the ax from him and cut several smaller trees to use for crosspieces. He got Dunklee's blankets from behind his saddle.

Now, with Franks's rope, with the poles and blankets, with leather strips cut from the rear cinch of his own double-rigged saddle, he made a travois. After saddling Dunklee's horse, he lashed it in place. The animal fidgeted, not liking the contraption, but Emmett Franks held him with an unyielding hand.

Dolan said, "Climb in, Mr. Dunklee, and you'll get a chance to see how the Indians ride."

Dunklee glanced at him suspiciously to see if the sheriff was making fun of him. Apparently deciding he was not, he climbed gingerly into the travois, bracing his feet against the lower crosspiece. His weight made the blankets sag but not far enough to touch the ground. He grinned at Dolan and sighed with relief.

Dolan grinned back. "Feels better already, huh?" He turned to the others. "Saddle up and let's get out of here."

He saddled his own horse, then took the reins of Dunklee's horse while Franks saddled his. Sam Joseph led out at a trot, still leading the pack animals, speeding up when Dolan called, "Gallop. We'll have to push 'em hard."

Dolan rode immediately behind the Negro, dragging Dunklee's horse along. The animal was skittish about the pole contraption dragging from his saddle, and once he tried to kick it off. His hoofs only struck a travois crosspiece and bounced off harmlessly.

The trail wound, seemingly endlessly, down long sagebrush-covered slopes into shallow draws, then up other slopes, across other ridges, down into other draws. Sometimes the trail skirted a precipitous rim for half a mile or so. Again, it wound through a thick pocket of spruce and pine or through a grove of aspen trees.

The travois skidded along, raising a cloud of dust. Dolan slowed when he saw that Daybright and Franks were eating dust, and let them go ahead. Once he called back to Dunklee, "How is it going, Mr. Dunklee?"

"Fine, except that I feel like a squaw."

"Better that than the way you felt before." He was trying not to let his worry show, but he was scared. Aragon had Flora Doniphan, and Dolan could remember very clearly the way he had looked at her. She'd get no consideration from Aragon. Saying no to Aragon wouldn't do her a bit of good.

Nor was Flora Doniphan his only worry. He was also worried that by the time they got to J Diamond, Aragon, Sims and Grogan would be gone, with all the fresh horses Jack Diamond had. They'd have a good five-hour start.

And even if he did eventually catch up, he'd have to fight Aragon again to bring him under control. He stared at Sam Joseph's back, ahead. Sam wasn't going to forgive Aragon for insulting him either. Not in a million years.

His thoughts turned to Flora Doniphan for a time. He remembered her face and the way she held her head. He remembered the way her hand had sometimes come up to brush back a wisp of hair. He wondered if Doniphan had appreciated her and then promptly called himself a fool for wondering. Of course Doniphan had appreciated her. Otherwise he wouldn't have married her.

He thought back along the years, remembering his own wife and the year they'd shared before she died. He had sometimes wished they'd had children. He had often wished that he had married again. He could have married again if he had tried.

He admitted now that the reason he hadn't wasn't the reason he'd given himself at the time. He had told himself that he'd never find another woman like Elizabeth. But the real reason had been that he couldn't tolerate the thought of losing another wife. The pain of losing Elizabeth had been too terrible.

From its zenith overhead, the sun began to advance toward the west. The heat increased. Dust from the horses ahead of him choked Dolan's nostrils.

This part of the plateau was unfamiliar to Dolan. The land went on and on ahead with a certain monotonous sameness.

Often they startled deer. Occasionally they saw a horse or a small band of them. They could be horses belonging to Jack Diamond, thought Dolan, or they could be wild. There were a lot of wild horses in Utah, and some of them might have strayed up here.

Sam Joseph halted to rest the horses. Dolan looked back at Dunklee. The man seemed comfortable. Dolan realized that it was almost midafternoon. Aragon, Sims and Grogan would be arriving at J Diamond soon. The thought infuriated him.

He rode ahead and handed the reins of Dunklee's horse to Daybright. He rode up beside Franks. "You know this country, Emmett. Isn't there a quicker way of getting there?"

Franks gestured with his head at a yawning canyon on the left. "There's an old Ute trail down through the rim. It climbs out on the other side. It cuts off about twelve miles because otherwise we've got to go around the head of this canyon to reach J Diamond on the other side."

"Why can't we go down the trail?"

"Too treacherous. The trail was in pretty fair condition when the Utes were using it all the time, but since they've been penned up on the reservation, it's gone all to hell. It's washed out, and in places you can't even find the damn thing because of the way the shale has slid over it."

"Could one man make it, do you think?"

"If he knew the trail he might."

"You mean you could."

Franks said doubtfully, "Maybe. But I sure as hell ain't anxious to give it a try."

"I wouldn't ask you to. I was thinking about me. Could you tell me enough about it so that I'd have a chance of making it?" He was silent a moment. Then he said bluntly, "The truth of the matter is, Aragon and those other two are going to be gone by the time we get to Diamond's place. We may never see 'em again. I figure Aragon's thinking of catching those bank robbers and taking the money for himself."

Franks shook his head. "I couldn't tell you enough about that trail so you could make it, Webb. But I suppose I could go with you."

His voice was so reluctant that Dolan didn't press. He waited and finally said, "It's up to you, Emmett. I want to catch Aragon, but I don't want to kill anybody doing it."

Franks made up his mind suddenly. He said, "Oh hell. Let's go."

Dolan road ahead to where Sam Joseph was. "Franks and I are going to take a short cut off this rim and up on the other side. You stay with the trail, and I'll see you at J Diamond tonight. Keep together and watch out for those Utes."

The tracker nodded. Dolan looked at Emmett Franks, who was still frowning doubtfully. "Let's go, Emmett. If it looks too tough, we'll turn around and come back."

Franks grinned ruefully. "Once you get on that trail you can't turn around." He headed down through the timber toward the rim.

CHAPTER EIGHT

THE OTHERS WERE almost immediately lost to sight, but for several moments Dolan could hear the travois poles dragging along the ground. Down here the smell of pine was strong and needles were deep and yielding underfoot.

Franks followed the draw straight down toward the rim. There was a small stream of water running in the draw, and after several minutes of riding, Dolan could hear it tumbling off the rim ahead.

The yawning canyon was already visible through the trees, dropping away from the level of the plateau by almost three thousand feet.

Apparently deer often used this trail. Their tracks were thick in it. And here, above the rim, the trail was damp and soft and fairly well defined. But Dolan knew it wouldn't stay that way. This trail had to descend through fifty to a hundred feet of sheer rimrock, and it would neccessarily be a narrow shelf trail where it did.

Steeper and steeper the trail descended, until at last there was nothing ahead but a yawning drop. Franks stopped his horse. He dismounted on the uphill side of the trail and said, "We'd better lead the horses down through the rim. It's too narrow for a man to ride. You scrape your leg against the rocks."

Dolan dismounted immediately. Franks went on ahead, leading his horse. Dolan followed, fifteen or twenty feet behind.

Following the stream, the trail descended through a fissure water had cut in the rim. Frank's horse was scrambling now, sliding on his haunches while Franks ran to stay out of his way ahead. Dolan stopped before he reached the steepest part and waited until Franks took the first switchback and came past going the other way thirty feet below. He didn't want to kick rocks down on Franks and his scrambling horse.

When Franks reached the next switchback, he stopped and yelled up to the sheriff, "Come on, Webb."

Dolan started down the trail. His horse balked, pulling back against the reins. Dolan went to him and stroked his neck, speaking soothingly. He thought fleetingly that the horse had better sense than he did.

He pulled again on the reins, but again the horse fought back. From below, Franks called, "Drag him, Webb. Once he starts down he'll be all right."

Dolan put his weight against the reins and literally dragged the horse onto the steepest part of the trail. Below, he could see Franks waiting, and beyond he could see a sheer drop of two hundred feet to the scattered rocks below. If the damn horse continued to fight and as a result lost his footing. . . .

The horse came forward suddenly, scrambling in terror down the trail. Dolan fell and nearly went over the edge. He caught himself, glanced up and saw his horse sliding toward him, trying to stop but unable to. If he didn't get out of the way. . . .

Desperately, he fought to his feet and clawed his way down the trail, sometimes stumbling, but managing to stay out of the horse's way. He reached the switchback and skidded around the turn.

His horse, coming on behind, sliding, scrambling, made a desperate effort to negotiate the turn. Dolan tried to help by hauling on the reins, literally pulling the horse's head around.

One of the horse's front feet went over the edge. He was on his haunches now, fighting, his eyes wide and rolling with his fright. He nickered shrilly with pure terror as the other front foot went off the edge.

Still Dolan tried to hold him, laying his whole weight back against the reins. The horse teetered over the brink, lost and knowing it, but still fighting desperately to regain his footing and save himself.

Below Dolan, Franks bawled, "let go, you fool! He'll drag you with him!"

But Dolan held on stubbornly. He'd had this horse since the animal was a three-year-old. They'd traveled a lot of miles together. They had been together a lot of years.

His feet went out from under him suddenly. Still holding the reins, he skidded toward the precipice.

The horse was already over. There was no use holding on. He released the reins, rolled and clawed at the sliding rocks with his bare fingers trying to keep from following the horse. His feet and lower legs went over the precipice, dangling in empty space. . . .

But suddenly he stopped. His fingers had found purchase on some solid rock and stopped his sliding body just in time.

Carefully, carefully, he pulled himself back onto the trail. He heard his horse's body hit the rocks below, with a sound he'd never be able to describe if he lived a hundred years. Sweating and trembling violently, he got cautiously to his feet. He looked at

Franks, waiting ahead of him on the next switchback below.

His knees were shaking. He saw that Franks was shaking, too. He managed a pallid grin. "Jesus Christ, I hope I never come that close again!"

Franks nodded. "Sit down and rest a minute!"

Dolan shook his head. "Huh uh. Let's get the hell off this damn trail. I can sit down when we've done that."

Franks nodded and led his horse on down the trail. Dolan followed cautiously. Damn Aragon to hell, he thought. The man had now cost him a good horse, a rifle and a saddle, too. The marshal was going to have a lot to account for when he caught up with him, if he ever did.

Down, down went the trail. Franks's horse, more surefooted than Dolan's horse had been, picked his way daintily, keeping the reins slack.

They negotiated the rim and crossed the shaly slide, now on a trail that at times was almost obliterated by sliding shale, at times almost entirely washed out by rain. Twice Franks's horse slipped, twice he recovered his footing and went on.

At last they came off the slide into a series of rounded, cedar-covered hills, and not long after that, came to the place where Dolan's bloody, dusty horse lay among the jagged rocks.

The horse was dead. The saddle tree was shattered, the leather literally ripped from the tree by the horse's fall. The rifle had disappeared. There was nothing worth salvaging but blankets and saddlebags. He recovered them and handed them up to Franks, who said, "Climb up behind," and gave Dolan a stirrup with which to mount.

Dolan swung up behind the man. Franks trotted the horse down through the cedars to the creek, where he allowed him to drink sparingly. Then the horse splashed across and began to climb out on the other side.

Stopping often to rest the horse, they rode up through the cedar-covered hills. Where the trail began its long ascent of the shale slide to the rimrock high above, Dolan dismounted and so did Franks. Leading the horse, Franks went on ahead, once calling back, "It's not far now, Webb. J Diamond isn't over a couple of miles from the head of the trail."

Dolan didn't reply. He trudged along behind Franks's horse, sweating heavily and breathing hard. In his thoughts he was steadily cursing Aragon. He was promising himself that someday, when the bank's money had been recovered and the outlaws caught, he and Aragon were going to have it out. He smiled faintly to himself, thinking how it would feel to smash a fist squarely into Aragon's mouth.

Dolan was thinking how Aragon must hate him just for being present on the afternoon of the robbery. If he hadn't happened to be in Pagosa, then the whole show could have been Aragon's. He could have selected a posse and taken it out himself. He would have been in full command.

Ahead of Dolan, dust raised from the horse's hoofs. Where the trail was excessively steep, Dolan grabbed hold of the horse's tail and let the animal pull him along. He lifted his glance toward the rims high above. He glanced at the position of the sun.

It must be close to three o'clock right now. Inside, he began to fume. He yelled, "Emmett, we're running out of time."

At a spot where brush grew below the trail, stablizing it, Franks stopped suddenly. He said, "Take the horse, Webb. I'll come on foot. You won't have any trouble finding J Diamond once you get out on top. Turn right at the top of the ridge and follow that two-track road. It goes straight to J Diamond. It's only about a mile."

Dolan hesitated briefly. Then he nodded, took the reins from Franks and swung to the horse's back. The horse moved on up the trail, leaving Emmett Franks behind. Looking back, Dolan saw him raise a hand and heard him call, "Good luck. I hope you get there in time."

He kicked the horse's sides. His own rifle had been lost when his horse tumbled off the trail, but Franks's rifle was here in the saddle scabbard. He pulled it out and levered open the breech. Satisfied that it was fully loaded, he let the hammer down to half cock and replaced the rifle in the boot.

Riding along, he mused bitterly on what a hell of a way this was to run a posse. He was here, alone. Franks was back on the trail about half a mile, also alone. Across the canyon were Sam Joseph and Daybright, with Dunklee riding a travois like a squaw. At J Diamond were Aragon, Sims and Grogan and the woman, Flora Doniphan. Somewhere, probably well behind, there were six angry Utes, one of whom had a splitting, aching head. And six or eight hours ahead were the three outlaws they were following, carrying eight thousand dollars in cash belonging to the bank. If he didn't succeed in recovering it, the bank might very well go broke. A lot of people could lose everything they had.

Irritably, he kicked the horse's sides, even though he knew the horse was going just as fast as he could. He crossed a long expanse of shale, negotiated a sharp switchback and finally began the long climb through the rim.

This rim was neither as high nor as sheer as the one on the other side. In addition, the horse had an advantage going up in that his footing was more secure. Dolan rode as far as he could, but when his leg scraped painfully against the rock, he raised it and hooked it around the horn the way a woman does with a sidesaddle, and at the first chance afterward dismounted and led the horse.

Water seeped out at the crown of the rim. The trail left the rocks at last and began its long climb through the timber toward the top of the ridge.

Dolan remounted and kicked the horse ugently, trying to make him trot despite the steepness of the trail. He was very much aware that a few minutes could mean the difference between failure and success. If he arrived to find Aragon and his two sidekicks gone, to find all of Jack Diamond's horses also gone, then his chance of ever catching them would be remote.

The horse kept slowing to a walk, and at last Dolan resigned himself to that pace. The horse plodded to the top of the ridge, where Dolan turned him right. Here, where the road was flat and level, he once more forced the horse to trot.

The road dipped into a long gully, then ascended a shallow ridge on the other side. At the top of this ridge, where a grove of aspens bordered it, Dolan caught a glimpse of the J Diamond buildings immediately ahead.

There was a two-story house, built of hand-hewn logs. There was a barn, built of aspen logs, chinked with mud. There was a corral, an outhouse and another small log building that was probably a chicken house. In front of the corral were several men, three of whom Dolan recognized as Aragon, Grogan and Sims. They were leading horses through the gate.

Dolan had already kicked his horse into a steady gallop down the slope. As he thundered along, he yanked the rifle from the saddle boot. He'd never stop Aragon with words. He knew that as surely as he had ever known anything. Furthermore, if Aragon ever got mounted—if he ever got a start—he'd be gone for good. There were no more fresh horses in the J Diamond corral. There were only the four worn-out ones that Aragon, Sims, Grogan and Flora Doniphan had ridden here.

Now only three hundred yards separated Dolan from the three. Aragon was trying to force Flora Doniphan to mount her horse. Dolan saw him slap her forcefully on the side of the face. After that, she mounted obediently.

A slow, smoldering fury kindled itself in him. He realized that his jaws were clenched. It felt as if every bit of blood had drained out of his face.

Aragon whirled his horse so savagely that the animal reared and nickered shrilly with fright. Sims and Grogan rode out of the yard, and Aragon followed, after giving Flora Doniphan's horse a cut across the rump with his rifle barrel.

Dolan yanked his running horse to a halt. He flung himself from the saddle and hit the ground. He skidded to a halt and quickly knelt.

The range between him and Aragon was now close to two hundred yards. He was unfamiliar with Frank's gun. But it was now or never, and at least he was on the ground where he could steady himself before he shot.

He thumbed the hammer back to full cock and squeezed the trigger carefully. The gun recoiled. Before he saw if the bullet had struck, he levered in another shell. Again he drew a careful bead and squeezed the trigger deliberately.

This time he saw the effect of his bullet instantly. The horse Aragon was riding dropped his head. He went to his knees, then somersaulted forward, rolling and raising a blinding cloud of dust. Aragon sailed out of the saddle and hit the ground.

Dolan was up and running. He paid no attention to Grogan or to Sims. They wouldn't go on without Aragon.

He was running straight toward Aragon and he was mad. He was mad enough to kill the man if he so much as offered to get up and fight.

CHAPTER NINE

DOLAN WAS LESS than fifty yards away before the marshal stirred. When Aragon came to his knees, hand poised over his holstered gun, Dolan skidded to a sudden halt.

Aragon got slowly to his feet. Dolan glared at him, poised and tense himself, and said wickedly, "Go ahead. Draw it! Let's settle this right now once and for all!"

The only sounds were those made by the horses. Sims and Grogan sat their saddles, frozen, seemingly afraid to move. Flora Doniphan had slid to the ground when Aragon's horse went down. Now she watched with horrified fascination the duel that was shaping up. Jack Diamond, short, wizened and rawhide-tough, glanced from Aragon to the sheriff and back again, his face neutral but hardly disinterested.

Dolan snapped, "Go ahead! I don't want to stand here all day!"

Aragon's glance darted toward Flora Doniphan. It shifted back to Dolan defiantly. Dolan could almost see the thoughts that were going around in the marshal's head. Aragon had been defeated by less than a minute in time, and that infuriated him. Furthermore, if he didn't draw his gun, he would be humiliated in front of Flora Doniphan. He would have to explain his failure to fight to Sims and Grogan if he was to continue to command their respect.

But he also knew that if he did go for his gun, he might end up dead. He was afraid of Dolan. He had been afraid ever since yesterday morning when Dolan roped him and dumped him out of his saddle onto the ground.

Aragon let his shoulders slump. He growled with plaintive defensiveness, "What the hell's eatin' you anyhow? All we was doing was trying to catch them goddam bank robbers. I figured you was a long ways back." He let his gun hand drop limply to his side.

Dolan said evenly, "You're lying! Neither you nor those other two had any intention of coming back once you got your hands on the money they took. That's why you left everybody else behind. Well let me tell you this, Aragon, once and for all. If you try that again, I won't shoot your horse. I'll shoot you right in your stupid head."

The placating smile left Floyd Aragon's face. His eyes narrowed and his mouth drew tight. Dolan said, "I'll take that gun. Just lift it out of the holster with a thumb and forefinger and let it drop on the ground."

Aragon hesitated briefly, then followed Dolan's instructions. Dolan said harshly, "Kick it away."

Aragon did. Dolan took the handcuffs out of his hip pocket and advanced toward Aragon. He said, "Turn around."

Scowling, Aragon obeyed. Dolan snapped a cuff onto his right wrist. He said, "Walk over there to the porch."

Aragon shuffled to the porch. Swiftly, Dolan pulled the handcuff chain around one of the supporting posts and locked the second cuff to Aragon's other wrist. The marshal was now secured to the post with his hands behind his back.

Dolan walked out into the yard and picked up the marshal's gun. "I won't be so quick to give this back to you next time."

He turned his back on Aragon and stared at Sims and Grogan, sitting their saddles uneasily. "I ought to send you two back. If it wasn't for those Indians, I would."

Neither of them replied. They watched him sullenly. He growled, "Put your horses into the corral."

They dismounted and led their horses and Flora Doniphan's to the corral. Dolan walked to Jack Diamond, who was grinning at him, and stuck out his hand. "I guess I haven't met you before, Mr. Diamond. I'm Webb Dolan." Diamond gripped his hand. Dolan asked, "Did Aragon pay you for the horses?"

Diamond shook his head. "Said the county would pay for 'em."

"All right. We'll leave it that way. Got any more?"

"I can have some here by dawn."

Dolan nodded. "All right." He studied Diamond briefly, then asked, "Those bank robbers come through here?"

"Yep."

"Give 'em fresh horses?"

"Didn't have no choice. They put guns on me."

"Pay you for 'em?"

"Nope. Told me to go to hell. I was gettin' ready to go after 'em when your men showed up."

Dolan said, "I'll see you get your horses back. Unless you want to come."

Diamond gestured with his head toward Aragon. "With him along? Not me, Sheriff. I'd rather lose the horses."

"How long ago did the bank robbers leave?"

"Two. Maybe a little after. One of 'em is hurt pretty bad. Delirious."

"Then they'll probably camp early tonight."

"I figure."

Dolan glanced toward the house. Aragon sat there with his hands behind him, his back against the post. He glared steadily at the sheriff, a sullen promise in his eyes. Dolan growled to himself, "Don't look at me that way. You had your chance."

He was thinking that if Aragon and his two cronies had managed to continue the pursuit, the outlaws would probably have seen them and traveled all night, lengthening their lead to more than fourteen hours by dawn tomorrow. As it was, they'd probably camp and remain less than six hours ahead.

He said, "We need eight fresh horses, Mr. Diamond. Could you possibly have them here by dark?"

Diamond nodded. "If I start right now I could."

"All right. Start now, then. I'll see that nobody bothers anything."

Diamond nodded. He went to the corral and caught up one of the horses Sims and Grogan had just turned in. He saddled, mounted and rode out without looking back. Dolan watched him approvingly. Diamond would have the horses here by dark. He was willing to bet on it.

He walked to where Flora Doniphan was standing. "I'm sorry you had such a bad time with Aragon, but I didn't have much choice about going back. Those Indians had Mr. Dunklee pinned down in some rocks, and if we hadn't got there when we did, they'd have killed him sure."

She looked at him for a moment, an unreadable expression in her eyes. Then she said, "It's not the first time a man ever hit me, Mr. Dolan. You've probably guessed—I worked in a saloon before I married Mr. Doniphan."

"Did he know?"

She nodded, meeting his glance steadily. "He knew. And he was never able to forget."

Dolan said shortly, "He was a fool."

He was startled to see a flush creep into her face. For an instant her eyes showed him her pleasure and her mouth curved into a faint, surprised smile. Then anger touched her expression and she turned away.

Dolan stared after her, frowning, wondering what had so suddenly angered her.

Franks walked over the ridge and plodded down into the yard. He looked at Aragon, handcuffed to the porch support. He glanced at Sims and Grogan, lounging sullenly nearby, then at Aragon's dead horse. He grinned at Dolan. "Looks like you got here just in time."

Dolan nodded. Franks studied him a moment, then walked to where Dolan had left the horse. He led him to the corral, unsaddled and turned him in. The horse immediately went to the hollowed-out-log water trough and began to drink. Franks tossed his saddle up onto the top rail of the corral, then turned to ask, "Are we going to be able to get fresh horses here?"

"Diamond's gone after them. He says he'll have them here by dark."

Franks nodded. Dolan walked to where Flora Doniphan was sitting dejectedly on a chopping block. "Would you mind fixing a meal for us?"

"I'll be glad to." She got up at once. Dolan said, "Maybe I could help."

"You could build up the fire in the stove."

He followed her into the house, shook down the ashes and rebuilt the fire in the stove. He sat down and watched her work, trying to figure out what had angered her so suddenly a few minutes before.

He was surprised at the amount of pleasure he

derived just from watching her. Once she turned and caught his glance and quickly looked away.

To bridge the sudden awkwardness, Dolan asked, "Would you rather stay here with Diamond and Mr. Dunklee until we get back, or would you rather go on with us?"

"I . . ." She hesitated, then turned her head to look squarely at him. "I'll stay if you want me to. I don't want to be any more burden than I already am."

He thought of the six Utes, one of whom was wounded and therefore doubly dangerous. If Flora stayed here, so would the Utes. They'd hang around, hoping to catch Diamond and Dunklee off guard or hoping to catch Flora Doniphan alone. Dolan knew he'd worry about her if he left her. He also knew that if anything happened to her, he'd never forgive himself. He said, "I'd rather you went with us."

"Then I'll go with you. I think I'd like that better anyway."

She went about her work efficiently. Dolan got up and went outside. He heard horses approaching and turned his head to see Sam Joseph and Daybright riding down off the ridge. Daybright was leading Dunklee's horse, still with the travois dragging along behind.

Daybright went to the corral and began to unsaddle. Dunklee climbed out of the travois and, limping, began to remove it and to unsaddle his horse. Sam Joseph rode to the porch and stared down at Aragon with narrowed, hate-filled eyes. He said softly, "Looks like you didn't make it, Mr. Aragon."

"Shut up, black man, and get out of here."

Dolan walked over and put himself between Aragon and Sam. "Go unsaddle your horse, Sam."

Sam rode toward the corral without looking back. Dolan said, "What I ought to do is turn him loose on you. Bare hands. You keep crowding and maybe that's what I'll do."

"I'll kill him if he steps in my way."

Dolan couldn't resist asking, "Like you did me a few minutes ago? Or will you shoot *him* in the back?"

Aragon's eyes were murderous. Dolan knew he was making a mistake in baiting Aragon. Aragon was already dangerous enough. Briefly he considered leaving the man behind, handcuffed and in Jack Diamond's custody. It was what Aragon deserved, but he knew it wouldn't be fair either to Diamond or Dunklee. Besides, there was a chance Aragon might escape.

Flora Doniphan came to the door. "Dinner's ready, Mr. Dolan."

"All right." He yelled to the men that there was food in the house. He walked to the spring and washed his hands and face. Then he went inside.

He sat down and, as soon as the others had arrived, began to eat. Sam Joseph had seated himself across the table from him. Dolan stared at Sam a moment, then said, "Diamond says those three bank robbers left here around two. He says one of them is hurt pretty bad. Both he and I believe they'll stop for the night, since they have no idea how close we are. Do you think you could take one of those fresh horses in the corral and trail them and find out where they camp? If you could do that, we could travel all night and be there when they break camp tomorrow."

Sam Joseph nodded. "I could try, Mr. Dolan."

Dolan nodded. Sam Joseph finished eating, got up and went outside. Moments later, Dolan heard his horse thunder out of the yard.

He pulled his watch from his pocket. It was four o'clock. Sam had about four hours before dark. But the outlaws had already been gone a little more than two hours. If he was going to catch them, he'd have to make that up. Or they'd have to make an early camp.

There was a chance that Sam would be able to make up enough time to discover where they camped for the night. He could then return, probably arriving back here a little after ten. The posse, if it left immediately afterward, could be at the outlaw's campsite when it got light. This chase could be ended. The money could be recovered. The posse could return here with the prisoners, catch up on lost sleep and head back for Pagosa by noon tomorrow.

It sounded tidy and neat, and Dolan hoped it would work out that way. But somehow, he couldn't make himself believe it would.

CHAPTER TEN

When Dolan finished eating, he got up. Flora was standing beside the stove. He said, "if you'll fix a plate for Aragon, I'll take it out to him."

She grinned at him unexpectedly. "I'm tempted to put rat poison into it."

He grinned back. It was the first time he had seen her smile, and he was startled at how beautiful she really was. She turned her back and fixed Aragon a plate. She got a tin cup and filled it with coffee. Dolan took plate and cup from her and carried them outside. He put them down, then unlocked Aragon's right wrist. He passed the empty handcuff around the post and relocked it to the chain, thus securing the marshal by his left hand, which he could now maneuver around in front of him.

He handed Aragon the plate and cup. He could feel the marshal's stare and said softly, "Glaring at me won't get you a thing. If you're tempted to do something about it, do it. Don't just sit there looking at me."

He half expected Aragon to throw the plate of food into his face. He sat down on a bench and watched Aragon. The rest of the men lounged around the yard. Dunklee was still limping, but he looked better than he had yesterday.

Aragon finished eating. Dolan took his plate and cup back inside the house. He handed them to Flora, who was washing dishes, then picked up a flour-sack towel and began to dry for her. She glanced at him and said, "Mr. Aragon said he was town marshal of Pagosa. Is that the truth?"

Dolan nodded, grinning faintly. "There are only a hundred and seventeen people in the town."

She glanced at the door. "He frightens me."

Dolan nodded. "You stay scared of him. He's dangerous."

She glanced again at the door. Dolan could see the fear in her face, but he could see anger there as well. She asked softly, "What are you going to do with him?"

"I haven't decided. Dunklee will have to stay here with Jack Diamond, and I've thought about leaving Aragon with them, but I don't suppose it's fair to ask either Dunklee or Diamond to take my troubles on. Besides, Aragon might get away."

"Wouldn't he just go back to town?"

Dolan shook his head. "It's gone too far between him and me. Now, he's got to show me up. Yesterday I roped him and dumped him from his saddle and clipped him on the side of the head with my gun. Today I shot his horse out from under him and handcuffed him to that post. He probably figures he can't go back to Pagosa until he evens things up with me."

"Do you live in Pagosa, too?"

He shook his head. "No. I live at the county seat. Mesa."

"How did you happen to be in Pagosa when the bank was robbed?"

"I was there to serve a summons. I saw the whole thing from about half a mile away."

"Mr. Aragon said they killed a little girl."

He nodded. "Cal Daybright's girl. She was only seven years old."

"That's awful. How did it happen?"

"She ran in front of them. It was an accident, but that doesn't make it any easier for Cal and his wife to bear. Susan was their only child."

Her eyes rested steadily on his face. "You've got a lot more to worry about than just catching the men who robbed the bank, haven't you?"

He grinned wryly. "I sure do. I'm afraid Daybright might try taking the law into his own hands when we catch up. I'm half afraid Aragon and his two sidekicks may try for the money. And then there's always that bunch of renegades."

"And me. I don't make things any easier."

He looked straight at her. "No. But I'm sure enjoying your company."

She flushed and glanced away.

He asked bluntly, wanting to know this now. "How did you happen to marry Doniphan?"

Her eyes sparkled, and for a moment he thought she was going to tell him it was none of his business. Instead she said, "He wanted someone to keep house for him, and I wanted to get out of the saloon and be respectable. I guess you could say we married for the wrong reasons, but he got his house taken care of and I got out of the saloon. We both got what we wanted. I wonder why neither of us was satisfied."

Dolan said softly, "Marriage is more than a business arrangement."

She nodded. "I know that now. I guess I thought the other things would come. Only they never did." She studied him a moment, smiling slightly. "You have the look of a bachelor. Are you?"

He nodded. "How can you tell?"

"I don't know. Maybe it's an independent look. Or

maybe it's the way an unmarried man looks at a woman that gives him away."

Dolan said, "I was married once. She died after about a year."

"I'm sorry."

"No need. It was a long time ago."

"It still hurts, though, doesn't it?"

He nodded. "I suppose it does sometimes."

"And you've never married again? Why?"

He shrugged. He was about to give some noncommittal answer, but then he changed his mind. He said, "I guess it was cowardly. I was afraid. I didn't want to be hurt again." He paused a moment, and then said, "Besides, I guess I didn't expect I'd be able to find someone like her a second time."

Flora Doniphan began to put the dishes away. Dolan carried the dishpan to the door and emptied it. He took it back to her, but she didn't look at him.

He asked, "Do you know where you'll go from here?"

She said shortly, "Back to where I was when Mr. Doniphan married me, I suppose."

"I thought . . ."

"That I wanted to get away from the saloons? Well, I did, but it didn't work." Her eyes met his, and they were suddenly angry eyes. "Let me alone, Mr. Dolan. Just let me alone."

He hesitated only a moment. Then he went to the door and stepped outside. It wasn't the first time in his life that a woman had puzzled him. They had seemed to be getting along so well and suddenly . . .

He crossed to Dunklee. "Mr. Dunklee, I lost my saddle going down off the rim. Since you'll be staying here, I wonder if you'd let me borrow yours."

"Of course. Will Mrs. Doniphan be staying, too?"

"I don't know what Mrs. Doniphan is going to do." He realized that he sounded irritated and modified the statement. "But I think she'll be going on with the posse until we reach a town. Or until we reach someplace where she can be put on a stage."

"Aragon isn't going to let her alone."

"He'll let her alone or he'll tangle again with me."

"What if something should happen to you?"

Dolan frowned. He hadn't thought of that. He supposed he ought to think about it now. He'd already tangled with Aragon twice, and either encounter could have been fatal if things had happened to turn out a little differently. In addition, he had almost tumbled off the rim with his horse earlier today. There had been some risk involved in the encounter with the six Ute renegades.

He said, "Hell, Mr. Dunklee, I can't leave her here. Those Utes had a look at her, and they're not going to quit if they think there's a chance to get their hands on her. Besides, if I left her with you, the Utes wouldn't let any of you alone. They'd kill you both to get at her."

Dunklee's face was sober. He said reluctantly, "Then I guess you hadn't better leave her here. The Indians would treat her a hell of a sight worse than Aragon."

"I could leave Aragon instead."

Dunklee shook his head. "You'd have to leave him handcuffed like he is right now. Otherwise, he'd follow you."

Dolan shrugged. "I guess I'll have to take both him and Mrs. Doniphan." He left Dunklee and walked up the slope until he stood on the highest point of land. He stared gloomily toward the west.

From here, he could see the void that was the vast Utah desert as a flat horizon fifty miles away. He doubted if the three outlaws would try descending to the desert floor tonight. The trail leading down must be nearly twenty miles.

He sat down on a rock and rolled a cigarette. He inhaled, trying to calm his frayed nerves, trying to still the strange feeling of depression that had come over him. It was almost as if he had a premonition of disaster. It was almost as though he guessed something was going to happen to him.

He got up again and began to pace nervously back and forth. The sun slid down the sky toward that distant horizon, now almost hidden by a shimmering haze of heat. Down there, water would be a problem he didn't have up here. As if there weren't already problems enough.

He returned reluctantly to the house. He laid down in the shade and pulled his hat down over his face. He shut his eyes and tried to sleep, without success.

He kept seeing Flora Doniphan in his thoughts. He kept hearing her voice. He slept, at last, and he dreamed about Elizabeth. Somehow, in his dream, she and Flora Doniphan were one.

He awoke with a start. It was dark. Horses were thundering toward the corral, which Franks had opened. Jack Diamond finished pushing the horses he had gathered into the corral, then dismounted and closed the gate.

Dolan got up, rubbing the sleep out of his eyes. He was glad to have gotten a little rest. Aragon was still handcuffed to the post. He didn't see Flora Doniphan.

The noise had also awakened Daybright, Dunklee, Sims and Grogan. Dolan walked to the door of the house, a square of light in the darkness, and looked inside. Flora was sitting in a chair, rocking gently back and forth. She felt his glance and smiled at him. She said, "I was rude to you. I'm sorry."

"It's all right."

"Will we be leaving soon? I have coffee ready if anybody wants it."

"I'll tell the rest of them. I know I'd like a cup."

She got up immediately and poured a cup of coffee for him. Jack Diamond came in the door, and Dolan said, "Mrs. Doniphan used your provisions to fix a meal for us. Add it to the voucher you send in for the horses."

"I saw them Utes' tracks comin' in."

Dolan nodded. "I didn't figure they'd give up."

"You fixin' to take her along with you?"

Dolan nodded again. "I'd like to leave Mr. Dunklee here with you, if that's all right. He's too saddlesore to travel any more."

Diamond shrugged. "It's all right with me. I'll be here. I've got some broncs to break. Brought 'em in along with the horses I promised you."

"You won't need to worry about the Utes."

Diamond looked at Flora Doniphan. "I know."

She glanced from Dolan to Diamond and back again. "Do you mean they're after me?"

"I'm afraid they are. That's why I told you I'd rather you went with us."

Her face was pale. She said, "I'll be ready, Mr. Dolan, whenever you are."

He smiled at her and put his empty cup on the table. He went outside. He told the men she had coffee inside for them and watched them file into the house.

He walked to the corral and stared at the milling horses moodily. It was after ten. Sam Joseph ought to be getting back here soon. He had left at four. Assuming the outlaws had traveled until seven, Sam should have located their camp shortly after dark. If he had started back immediately, he ought to be getting here.

He could see the lumped shape that was Aragon sitting on the porch. He crossed to the man and stood looking down at him. "I'm going to let you go. I'm even going to let you come along. But next time I tangle with you, one of us is going to wind up dead. It isn't going to be me."

Aragon didn't answer him. Dolan said, "Damn you, answer me! Can you behave yourself, or do you want me to leave you locked to this post until we get back?"

Aragon growled, "I'll behave, Sheriff. I'll behave." Even if his tone hadn't been so grudging, Dolan wouldn't have believed him. He knew Aragon and knew exactly what to expect from him.

He got the handcuff key from his pocket, knelt and unlocked the cuff around the marshal's wrist. Aragon got up immediately, rubbing his wrist. Dolan said, "Mrs. Doniphan has coffee made inside. But you treat her with respect!"

Aragon glanced at him and, for a moment, Dolan thought he was going to say something. Aragon remained silent, though, and went sullenly into the house. Immediately, Daybright, Dunklee and Franks came out.

Dolan unlocked the other cuff and put the key into his pocket. He retrieved his saddlebags from the corner of the house where he had left them earlier and put the cuffs into them. He let Aragon's gun remain in the saddlebags. The man had his rifle and didn't need his revolver, too.

He heard a horse approaching and glanced up. Sam Joseph rode into the yard and stopped in the light streaming from the door. He said, "They camped early, Mr. Dolan, I guess because of that wounded man. I can take you right to their camp. I don't see no reason why we can't have it surrounded by daybreak if we start right away."

Dolan yelled, "All right, everybody! Saddle up and let's get out of here!"

CHAPTER ELEVEN

In darkness, the column moved out. Sam Joseph took the lead, waiting beyond the limits of Jack Diamond's yard for the others to take their places in line.

Dolan helped Flora Doniphan to mount, saying, "Stay ahead between Sam Joseph and me where I can keep an eye on you."

She looked down at him, her expression hidden by darkness. "Do you think you will catch them now?"

"We should. Sam knows where they're camped, and he says we can get there by the time it's light."

"And what will you do with me?"

"If we catch them, I suppose you had better come on back to Pagosa with us."

"You say, 'if we catch them.' Is there any doubt?"

Dolan grinned humorlessly in the darkness. "There's always doubt. They might hear us and get away. They might decide to shoot it out. Plenty of things can go wrong."

The others fell in behind. Dolan had made no attempt to take the pack horses and their load of oats. Diamond's horses weren't used to oats. They probably had never seen grain before, and he doubted if they would eat it. The horses they had ridden from town would remain at Diamond's place until the posse returned, by which time they would be sufficiently rested for the return trip.

Sam Jospeh rode confidently through the darkness. Glancing back, Dolan saw that Franks was immediately in back of him. He couldn't see the others well enough to recognize them but only as shapes silhouetted against the starlit sky.

He wondered what Aragon would try next. He refused to believe that his trouble with Aragon was over. He knew the man too well.

Occasionally now, a faint smell of perfume was carried back to him from Flora Doniphan, riding close ahead. He watched her even though he couldn't see her very well. And he made his mind up definitely about one thing. He wasn't going to let her go out of his life as easily as she had come into it. He was going to see her after they had returned to town. He would see her as often as possible, and after a decent period of time had passed . . .

He shook himself impatiently. He was daydreaming like a boy. And this was no time for that.

He wondered where the Ute renegades were and grinned faintly to himself. That was one advantage of riding out in the middle of the night. The Utes probably wouldn't even know they had gone until it got light tomorrow.

Intermittently, he dozed. Ahead, Flora also dozed occasionally. Once she nearly fell from her saddle but recovered herself in time, with a little cry of surprise. Only Sam Joseph, in the lead, remained alert.

Two hours passed, and another two, and at last, as dawn was beginning to darkly gray the eastern sky, Sam Joseph pulled his horse to a halt at the crest of a shallow rise.

The air by now was crisp and cold. Dolan was shivering. He pulled his horse up close beside Flora's and asked, "Are you all right?"

She nodded. His horse moved in closer, nuzzling her mount, and for an instant Dolan's leg touched hers. He felt it trembling from cold. He said, "As soon as the sun comes up, we'll get warm again."

She did not reply. Sam Joseph spoke to the clustered men. "They ahead, over the next ridge and down that draw leading away to the right. I think they's water in the draw, which is probably why they camped there, but I can't be sure. It don't matter anyway."

Dolan said, "You know the lay of the land. What's the best way of surrounding them? I don't want any shooting if it can be helped."

Sam said, "I can take three men and close off the lower end of the draw, the hillside beyond their camp, and the upper end of the draw. If you move in from this direction with the men you have left, I think maybe we can convince them to give themselves up without a fight."

Dolan nodded. He said, "Take Daybright and Franks. Grogan, you go with them, too. Sims, you and Aragon stay with me."

Keeping Aragon with him was the only way he knew of keeping the man under control. If he sent Aragon with Sam Joseph, the marshal would take charge the instant they were out of sight.

Sam moved away, followed by Franks and Grogan, then by Daybright. As the storekeeper went by, Dolan said, "There'll be no shooting unless it's necessary, Mr. Daybright. Do you understand? I'll hold you accountable."

Daybright didn't answer him. He moved off in the semi-darkness, hunched against the cold, but with an obvious tension in him that Dolan couldn't miss. He wished he was going to be with Daybright when the three outlaws were caught, but he knew it was more important that he stay with Aragon.

As the file of mounted men faded into the gloom, he turned his head toward Flora Doniphan. "Stay about fifty yards behind, Mrs. Doniphan. I don't want you with us if those three start shooting, but neither do I want you so far back that I can't see you."

"All right."

Dolan said, "We'll give Sam ten minutes to get set on the other side of the outlaws' camp. Then we'll move in. When we do, I want you on my right, Mr. Aragon, maybe fifty yards away. And you on my left, Mr. Sims."

Sims grunted something he couldn't understand. Aragon did not reply. Dolan turned around in his saddle and reluctantly got Aragon's gun out of his saddlebags. He handed it to the marshal, who shoved it into the holster at his side without comment.

When he judged the ten minutes were up, Dolan said softly, "All right, spread out. Keep a line and don't get ahead or fall behind."

By now the entire sky was gray. In the east, a few scattered clouds had turned pale pink. Birds were chirping in the brush and nearby aspen trees. It was so cold that Dolan could see his horse's breath.

He glanced around when they hit the little swale at the bottom of the rise. Flora Doniphan was coming along steadily about fifty yards behind, staying directly in back of him. When she saw him watching her, she raised a hand and smiled.

Dolan returned his attention to the ridge ahead. Glancing right, he saw that Aragon had drawn his gun. He slipped his rifle out of the saddle boot and slowly packed a cartridge into it, muffling the sound of the action with his other hand. He laid the gun muzzle in the crook of his left arm.

They were now halfway up the second rise. Dolan raised a hand and the trio stopped. He dismounted, beckoned to Flora and when she had caught up, handed her the reins. He motioned to Aragon and Sims to remain where they were, then went on afoot.

Nearing the crest of the rise, he moved with exaggerated care so that he would make no noise. Once he halted briefly to check the breeze, which fortunately was blowing from his left and would not, therefore, carry the smell of the horses to the outlaws' mounts down in the draw.

At last he could see their camp. Two of the outlaws were huddled over a small campfire that they apparently had just lighted. The third lay motionless not far away. Dolan wondered if the wounded man had died.

Apparently the outlaws were almost ready to leave. Their horses, saddled, stood nearby tied to clumps of brush. Dolan started to withdraw. If he and the two with him moved in carefully, they ought to be able to make it partway down the slope before they were seen. Sam Joseph and those with him ought to be within rifle range on the slope beyond, and up and down the draw.

He was no more than halfway to his horse when the shot rang out. He jumped with startled surprise, then yanked his head around and stared at Aragon, from whose direction the shot had come.

Aragon was looking at him sheepishly. He called, "I'm sorry, Sheriff. I had the hammer cocked and it just went off."

Dolan raced to his horse, cursing angrily beneath his breath. He knew the shot had been no accident. Aragon had deliberately warned the outlaws so that they could escape.

He snatched the reins out of Flora's hands and swung astride. He dug spurs viciously into the horse's sides, and the animal leaped away, digging in and running almost instantly. He raced toward the crest of the rise.

Dolan didn't give a damn whether Aragon and Sims were coming on behind or not. All he wanted was to get down into that outlaw camp. The outlaws' horses had been tied less than a dozen yards away from them. It would take no more than a few seconds for them to reach the horses, mount and race away. And then all the planning, all the long night of riding would be wasted, thrown away. Because of Aragon. Damn him. Damn him to hell!

He crested the rise. The camp below was empty except for the man who had been lying on the ground, now sitting up, a rifle in his hands. Dolan roared, "Drop it, damn you, or you're dead! You're surrounded and you haven't got a chance!"

He didn't wait to see if the man complied or not. Right now he didn't care about the wounded man. The other two were escaping, and they would have the eight thousand dollars belonging to the bank.

He could see them up the draw, their horses disappearing into the trees. He roared. "Hey! Up there in the draw! They're coming toward you!"

He raced in the direction the two had gone. He raked the horse's sides cruelly. And suddenly the half-broke animal began to buck.

Dolan yanked his head up angrily. Again he raked the horse's sides with his spurs. He heard a shot in the draw ahead, then a couple more, then a fourth. After that there was only silence.

He glanced around, wondering who was up there in the draw. He could see Sam Joseph on the other slope, and a hundred yards downcountry on the same slope, he saw Daybright. No one was visible in the lower draw.

He entered a grove of aspen trees, and his horse deliberately ran under a low branch, trying to brush him off. Dolan swung to one side, Indian fashion, clinging to the horse's neck with his arms, to the saddle with a leg hooked over it. He flung himself back into the saddle immediately.

Suddenly, in front of him, he saw Emmett Franks. Franks had a blood-soaked shoulder, and his face was white and drawn with pain.

Dolan wanted to go on. More than anything, he wanted to go on and try outrunning the two outlaws before they put any distance between themselves and the posse following.

With Emmett wounded, he could not. The outlaws would have to wait. He had caught them once. He could catch up with them again.

He yanked his horse to a halt and swung to the ground. Franks stared at him apologetically. "I'm sorry, Webb. I let them get away. But they came on me so fast, I just wasn't ready for them."

"Think you hit either one?"

Franks shook his head. "I don't think so, Webb. They hit me with their first shot. It knocked me down. I got off a couple of shots, but I'm pretty sure that they were wild."

Dolan yanked out his pocketknife and opened it. As carefully as he could, he slit Emmett Franks's shirt at the shoulder and peeled it away from the wound. He said shortly, "See if you can move your arm."

Franks moved his arm, his face turning white with pain. Beads of sweat popped out on his forehead. Dolan said, "At least it didn't hit the bone. And the bullet went on out. That damn thing is going to hurt you like hell for the next few days, but I don't think it's too serious."

Franks whole face was drenched with sweat. He said, "It's beginning to hurt already, Webb."

Dolan picked up his horse's reins. He found Franks's horse and untied him. Leading the two, he returned to Franks. "Can you walk?"

"Hell yes, I can walk. I can ride, too, as soon as I get this damn thing bandaged up."

Dolan nodded. "You'll have to unless you want to risk running into those renegade Utes back there."

He walked back down the draw, leading the two horses, staying close to Franks in case the man should need support. He was smolderingly furious at Aragon for deliberately firing his gun and giving the outlaws time to get away. But he knew Aragon would never admit it had been deliberate.

He scowled. They could have had the outlaws and the money and be getting ready to return to town tonight. Now the chase would have to go on and on, onto the desert and beyond. It was even possible that the bank robbers would get clean away.

But at least he had one of them, he thought. And he hadn't heard any shots back at the outlaws' camp, so Daybright hadn't killed the wounded outlaw yet.

CHAPTER TWELVE

In the outlaw's camp, the fire was just now beginning to burn well. There was a pot of coffee boiling on it. Sam Joseph, Aragon, Sims, Grogan and Daybright were there, their horses standing ground tied nearby. The wounded outlaw was still sitting up, but he no longer had his rifle. It lay a dozen feet away where he had thrown it when Dolan yelled at him.

Even from a distance of a hundred yards, Dolan could see that he was hardly more than a boy. He had long yellow hair and a fine growth of yellow whiskers on his face. His eyes were wide and scared, his face drawn and gray with pain.

Daybright stood no more than fifteen feet away from him, a rifle in his hands, pointed straight at the boy. Daybright's face was white, his lips compressed. His whole body was shaking—knees, shoulders, arms. There was pure agony in his eyes as he shouted at the wounded boy, "Damn you to hell! You killed her! You ran her down like she was nothin' but a dog!"

The boy raised his hands and covered his eyes, as though he could shut out the face of the outraged father. Dolan reached the group, for the moment forgetting Franks and his shoulder wound. He dropped a hand to his revolver, but he didn't draw it from its holster. He didn't want to spook Daybright. He didn't want to shoot the man in defense of a killer, an out-law, no matter what his age, but he knew he would shoot the storekeeper if it came to a choice between doing that or letting Daybright shoot the prisoner.

He said, "Cal, put down that gun. He ain't no more'n a boy."

Daybright didn't even look at him. In a low voice charged with passion he said, "He's old enough to kill. And damn him, I'm going to kill him like he killed her!"

Dolan looked beyond Daybright at the others. He couldn't depend on Aragon or on Grogan or on Sims. But he could depend on Sam if Sam could edge close enough to knock the barrel of Daybright's gun aside. He caught Sam's eye and nodded almost impercepti-bly. Sam took a slow, stealthy step toward Daybright, another and another still.

The boy took his hands away from his face. Trying to distract Daybright, Dolan asked, "What's your name, son?"

The outlaw tore his glance from Daybright and looked at him. "It's Willie, sir. Willie Brundage."

"You got folks, Willie? You got a home?"

The boy shook his head. Dolan could see now that he wasn't more than sixteen years old. He asked, "What happened to them?" He kept watching Day-bright out of the corner of his eye, hoping the ques-tions and answers would distract him, even momentar-ily, from what he meant to do. Sam Joseph was now no more than a dozen feet away.

"Pa died from a rattlesnake bite. I don't know what was wrong with Ma, but she died two months after-ward."

"Where was this?"

The boy gestured toward the west. "Over there."

"On the desert? What were you doing there?"

"Pa tried to farm. Our crops burned out."

"And when they died, what did you do then?"

"I didn't know what to do after I buried Ma. Then these two men showed up. They said I could come with them."

"So you went. What were their names?"

"Mr. Tharp. Herbie, the other one called him. And Mr. Foley. His first name was Ray."

"How many robberies were you in on before the one in Pagosa?"

"None. That one was the first."

"You held the horses. You know you're just as guilty as they are, don't you?"

"Yes, sir." Willie's words were hardly audible.

"And you know you're as guilty as they were of killing the little girl?"

Willie's expression was agonized. "I'm sorry, sir. I'm so awful sorry that I'd do anything to bring her back. I'd shoot myself." He looked at Daybright squarely. "I'll shoot myself if it will help. Or else you just go ahead. I deserve to be shot."

Sam had almost reached Daybright. Now Dolan shot him a warning glance. Daybright was wavering, and he would a lot rather see Daybright desist of his own free will than have Sam Joseph wrest the gun from him by force.

Sam Joseph stopped. Willie Brundage unexpectedly began to sob brokenly. Daybright lowered the gun. He looked helplessly at Dolan. "I can't do it, Webb. I can't shoot that kid."

"I didn't figure you could."

"What are you going to do with him?"

Dolan looked at the boy. "How bad is your wound?"

"It's in my leg. I guess I've lost a lot of blood, because I feel awful weak. I heard them talking about leaving me behind last night. They said I was slowin' them down too much."

"Did they take all the money, or did they leave you your share?"

"They said they'd keep it because the posse would catch me and take the money anyway. They said as soon as they could find out where I was, they'd send my share to me."

"You didn't believe that, did you?"

"No, sir. I knew I'd never see them again. I knew I'd get caught and either hanged or sent to jail."

Dolan nodded. Sam Joseph said, "I'll look at his wound, Sheriff, if you want me to. I ain't no doctor, but I know a little about doctorin' animals."

Dolan said, "Go ahead."

He turned away, frowning to himself. Willie Brundage was another problem—more trouble in a posse already loaded down with it. He remembered Franks's wound and turned back to Sam. "Soon as you get done with him, look at Mr. Franks. He needs bandaging."

But Flora Doniphan was already bandaging Emmett Frank's wound with strips she had torn from her petticoat. Franks's face was white, and he was swaying slightly. Dolan said, "Emmett, sit down." He reached the man just as Franks buckled. He caught him and eased him to the ground. Franks was still conscious but only barely so.

Dolan knew he was going to have to send Willie Brundage back to J Diamond, and he would have to send someone along with him. Franks could probably go with Brundage and whoever was assigned to accompany him. But if he lost Franks, and two others, probably Aragon and Daybright, the posse was going to be pretty shorthanded. Remaining would be only himself, Grogan, Sam Joseph and Sims.

Still, with both Daybright and Aragon out of the way, he'd have a lot better chance of catching the outlaws and returning the money to the bank. And four men ought to be enough to capture two.

Flora finished bandaging Emmett Franks while Dolan held him erect. Daybright brought a blanket and spread it, and Dolan eased Franks back onto it. He got to his feet. "Grogan, you and Sims make a travois to take Brundage back to J Diamond. Get busy with it. Every minute we waste here means those two outlaws are getting farther away."

Sam Joseph finished rebandaging the outlaw, then got up and went with the pair to help cut travois poles. Franks was fully conscious now. Dolan said, "You're going back. You can't go on with that shoulder wound."

Franks nodded reluctantly. "I thought I could keep going, but I guess I can't."

"Can you ride, or do you want a travois?"

Franks grinned. "I can ride."

"I'm going to send Aragon and Daybright back with you."

"For God's sake, why those two?"

"I want to get rid of Aragon. Daybright can watch him and see that he doesn't shoot Brundage and then say he was trying to escape. I want you to watch him, too."

"All right."

Dolan glanced around, looking for Aragon. The man was standing about fifty feet away, talking to Flora Doniphan. He was smiling ingratiatingly, but she was not smiling back.

Sam Joseph returned with Sims and Grogan, dragging travois poles and poles with which to make crosspieces. He immediately set to work making a travois for the wounded outlaw.

Dolan paced back and forth restlessly, thinking about the two escaping outlaws racing away toward the west. He wished he could get going, but he knew that too much haste right now might be wasteful in the end.

Flora looked uncomfortable and Dolan felt sorry for her, but she was keeping Aragon occupied. At last the travois was finished. Sam, upon instructions from Dolan, lashed it to the saddle of Daybright's horse. Dolan and Sam lifted Willie Brundage into it as gently as they could. Even so, he cried out from pain, turned white and began to sweat. He fainted before they had him settled. Sam Joseph lashed him in.

Dolan beckoned Daybright. "I want you to go back with him, Cal. I'm going to send Aragon along with you."

"Why me? You know how I feel about that damned kid."

"I know."

"You're afraid I might try to shoot those other two when we catch up with them, aren't you?"

Dolan nodded. "Maybe. You stopped yourself from shooting this one, but then he's only a kid. And hurt to boot."

"I've got a right to go with you."

Dolan shook his head. "You've got no rights. You stopped yourself from shooting Willie because he was wounded and because he was just a kid. But those other two—you might shoot one of them. And then I'd have to charge you with murder. I wouldn't have any choice."

Daybright nodded reluctantly. "I guess you're the boss."

"Good. I'm counting on you, now, to see that Aragon doesn't do anything to that kid."

"You don't think he'd . . ."

"I think Aragon is capable of shooting him and then saying he got a gun or was trying to escape. I don't want it to happen."

"All right. I'll keep an eye on him."

"Mount up, then. I'll get Aragon."

He walked to where Aragon was standing, talking to Flora Doniphan. He said, "I'm sending you back with Franks and Daybright and that wounded kid. Take them to J Diamond and wait for us. We shouldn't be gone more than a day or two."

"The hell! You're not sending me back! I'm going with you after those bank robbers."

Dolan smiled coldly. "Floyd, you sure as hell do tempt a man." He took a step away from Aragon. He saw the way the man's eyes flared. He said, "Flora, step aside."

She hastily moved aside. Dolan asked, "How's it going to be, Floyd? It don't make a damn bit of difference to me. But you're going back, unconscious, or dead, or riding your horse like the rest of them."

"How about when we get to J Diamond? Can I come back then?"

Dolan shrugged. "If you want to try catching up with us."

Aragon sullenly tramped away toward his horse. He mounted and scowled down at Dolan and at Flora Doniphan. "Why don't you send her back with us?"

Dolan didn't bother to answer him. He watched as Aragon led out, heading back toward J Diamond Ranch. Daybright followed, the travois with the outlaw riding it trailing behind his horse. Franks brought up the rear, riding in a twisted position, favoring his shoulder wound.

Once Aragon turned and glared back at him. Dolan returned his hostile stare steadily, and Aragon looked away.

Dolan helped Flora Doniphan to mount, then swung to his own horse's back. He said, "Lead out, Sam," and watched Flora move into position behind the Negro without being told. He swung in behind Flora. Behind him came Grogan and Sims.

Sam Joseph tunred his head. "Who fired the shot that warned them outlaws, Mr. Dolan?"

"Aragon. Who else?"

"You reckon it was an accident?"

Dolan shook his head. "Aragon didn't want those two caught. I figure he wanted them to stay free and in possession of the money until he could figure out a way of getting them himself."

"Then you don't reckon he'll stay at J Diamond?"

"Huh uh. He'll be back. But maybe by the time he catches up, we'll have the outlaws in custody and the money, too."

Sam's voice lowered, and he glanced beyond Dolan at Grogan and Sims, riding farther back. He said, "You reckon they're in it with Aragon?"

Dolan nodded. "They're in it all right. But they haven't got the guts to do anything without Aragon to back them up."

Sam Joseph nodded, turned and put his attention to the trail. They finally reached the last, high rim from which they could look ahead, out across the vast Utah desert, shimmering now in the midmorning sun.

Both Sam Joseph and Dolan squinted against the glare. Sam Joseph pointed, and Dolan stared steadily for a long time in the direction he indicated. At last he saw a lift of dust, and a moment later saw two tiny specks.

"That's them," Sam Joseph said. "They're just about an hour ahead of us." He put his horse into the trail leading down toward the sheer gray rim.

CHAPTER THIRTEEN

THE RIM WAS less precipitous here. As they descended, the heat increased steadily until, near the bottom, the air was like a furnace blast.

Dolan squinted against the glare and several times nearly choked on the fine alkali dust rising from the hoofs of Sam Joseph's and Flora Doniphan's horses just ahead.

The land was also different. It was dazzling white in the low spots where alkali lay like snow. The surface of the ground was gray elsewhere. And out of this gray, alkali soil grew only tall greasewood bushes that sometimes nurtured a small clump of grass in the shade they cast.

Sam Joseph trotted his horse for about a mile, then let him walk for another mile. After that he lifted him to a trot again.

Once Dolan called, "Are we gaining on them at all?"

Sam Joseph turned and shook his head. "Losin' ground, Mr. Dolan. But that's all right. They pushin' their horses too hard the way I look at it. In this heat, they pushin' their horses a heap too hard."

Dolan slumped uncomfortably in his saddle. He felt sorry for Flora Doniphan. She looked miserable. Her face was sunburned painfully and covered with

99

gray alkali dust. But when she occasionally turned her head to look at him, she smiled determinedly.

Every time they found a bit of shade cast by a towering rock or by a steep-walled arroyo, Sam Joseph rode to it and drew his horse to a halt. Each time he halted, he unsaddled and fanned his horse's overheated back with the saddle blanket. Dolan and the others followed suit. Flora Doniphan tried mightily to do her share, but usually all she managed was to get the saddle off before Dolan took over and helped her out.

Grogan and Sims were silent and sullen. Both kept watching the back trail as though they expected Aragon to appear.

Dolan also kept glancing back. He couldn't help himself. Like Grogan and Sims, he believed Aragon might appear at any time. He was sorry now that he had sent Willie Brundage back with Aragon, Daybright and Franks, because he knew Aragon was capable of killing Willie to be rid of him. And, Dolan decided reluctantly, he had been wrong in taking that kind of chance with Willie's life, even if he was an outlaw sure to be convicted and sent to jail.

He shrugged fatalistically. It was too late now to change anything. Besides, maybe he was wrong. Daybright and Franks were with Willie and Aragon. Daybright wouldn't allow Aragon to deliberately kill the boy. Nor would Aragon dare kill Willie as long as Daybright and Franks were witnesses.

Near six, they reached a stagnant, alkali water hole that the outlaws had deliberately muddied. They had ridden their horses back and forth through it until all that was left was black, foul-smelling mud. The horses went to it and put their muzzles in, sucking up the thin layer of water that had risen to the top. Dolan looked at Sam. "Is this going to hurt them?"

"Not unless they drink too much. A little ain't goin' to hurt."

"You figure those two outlaws will do this to every water hole?"

Sam nodded. "If they've got any sense, they will."

"You know this country, Sam?"

"Some. I been down this way two, three times, I guess."

"How scarce is water anyway?"

Sam Joseph shrugged expressively. "Depends, Mr. Dolan." He turned and pointed back at the towering plateau. "This time of year there's a lot of thunderstorms up there. The water runs down and fills up these dry washes here."

"What if they don't have any thunderstorms? Are there any creeks or rivers ahead of us?"

"A few. I don't figure we're goin' to die of thirst."

On and on the five plodding horses went. And ever stretching ahead of them was the trail of the two horses they were following. Dolan knew the outlaws would ride all night. They realized the posse was close behind. They also knew how difficult it would be for the posse to trail them in the dark. By tomorrow, instead of having an hour's lead, the outlaws would again be eight or ten hours ahead. Thanks to Aragon. Thanks to that deliberate warning shot.

But there was always the chance that something would happen to change things unexpectedly. One of the outlaws' horses might go lame. They might exhaust them by pushing them too hard.

Slowly, the sun sank toward the horizon straight ahead. Now it was a blinding glare in the eyes of the five dusty people riding toward it. Dolan tilted his hat forward. Flora Doniphan raised a hand.

Not a cloud marred the brassy-looking sky. Mirages shimmered ahead, hiding the desert, revealing it again. At last, mercifully, the sun sank out of sight.

At dusk they made a dry camp in the lee of a rocky butte. As he unsaddled, Dolan said, "The water in the canteens is all we have. I can't promise there will be any more when it's gone, so use it accordingly."

Flora had been about to moisten a handkerchief with water so that she could sponge her face. She changed her mind with an apologetic smile.

Sam Joseph was already gathering dry sticks of greasewood with which to build a fire. Dolan dumped part of the water in his canteen into a pan. He arranged some rocks around the fire so that the pan would heat. He dropped a handful of coffee in.

Sam Joseph, having built the fire, was now standing on a high point of land, staring back. Dolan asked, "See anything?"

"Dust."

"Aragon or the Indians."

"Not much dust, Mr. Dolan. Maybe Aragon."

"Have you seen any sign of those Indians today?"

"No, sir."

"You figure they've given up?"

"No, sir. They ain't givin' up. They know a dozen trails down off'n that mountain. They could be less'n a mile away right now."

"Then we'd better post a guard tonight."

"Yes, sir. That'd be a good idea."

He continued to stare back in the direction from which they had come. At last he said, "One man, Mr. Dolan. Too far away to tell, but I figure it's Mr. Aragon."

"Then Willie Brundage must be dead."

Flora, standing at Dolan's side, said softly, "He was pretty badly hurt. He had lost a lot of blood."

Sam Joseph said suddenly, "Two horses, Mr. Dolan. One's a ways behind the first one we saw."

Dolan said, "Daybright. Then it's pretty certain

that Willie's dead. They must have left Franks to go on alone."

He climbed up beside Sam Joseph and stared at the approaching horses. Both were coming on at a steady gallop. He cursed softly beneath his breath. Both horses would be played out. But he understood the two riders' haste. Aragon probably wanted to tell his story of Willie's death before Daybright arrived. And Daybright wanted to be on hand when Aragon told his story so that he could dispute its truth.

Dolan began to pace back and forth angrily. He had thought he was rid of both Daybright and Aragon. Now it looked as though he was going to have them both on his hands again.

Aragon pounded into camp. His horse was lathered. The marshal swung to the ground, and the horse stood still, quivering.

Dolan stared angrily at Aragon. He said, "You haven't had time to take Willie Brundage back to Jack Diamonds' place."

Aragon shook his head. He forced himself to meet Dolan's glance. "He tried to escape. He didn't give me no choice."

"So you shot him? Is that what you're trying to say?"

"I had to, Dolan. I said he didn't give me no choice."

"Oh sure not. A hurt kid that could hardly walk. He didn't have a gun, did he?"

"He got ahold of mine."

"Now how the hell did he manage that?"

"I leaned it against a tree. I didn't figure he could get off that travois, but he did. He got hold of that gun, and he was making for one of the horses."

Daybright rode into camp. It was now almost completely dark. Dolan couldn't see his face, but there was outrage and anger in the way Daybright held himself.

Dolan asked, "Well, what's your story, Cal? Aragon says Willie got hold of his rifle and was making for one of the horses when he shot him down."

"He's a liar. Willie couldn't hardly move. If he got hold of Aragon's rifle, it was because Aragon left it where he could."

"Did you see it, Cal?"

Daybright shook his head regretfully. "Aragon asked me to fetch some firewood."

"What for? What time was that?"

"Maybe five-thirty or six o'clock. He said we wasn't in no hurry, so we'd just as well take time to eat. I went off to gather some firewood. I heard a shot, and when I came back, Willie Brundage was dead. Shot right through the head."

"Where was Emmett all this time?"

"He laid down as soon as we made camp. He was pretty sick from riding a saddle all afternoon."

"So he didn't see anything either?"

"I guess not."

"Where was Willie when you arrived?" Dolan wished he could see Daybright's face. He also wished he could see the expression in Aragon's eyes.

"He was right there by the travois. No more'n ten feet away from it."

"And where was Aragon?"

"Right close. Fifteen or twenty feet away, I guess."

"Did Willie have a gun?"

"Not then he didn't. He was already dead when I arrived."

"Where was Aragon's rifle when you arrived?"

"Right beside Willie."

"In his hand? Under him?"

"Neither, I guess." Daybright's speech was slow as though he was trying to remember details that had already blurred in his mind. "I guess it was beside him. On the ground. Maybe a few feet away."

"How many feet? One? Three? Six?"

Daybright was silent for several moments, once more trying to remember and realizing the importance of his reply. Aragon growled, "What the hell are you trying to prove? That I murdered Willie? How do you figure you're going to prove a thing like that? Franks was out cold and had his back turned besides. Daybright was gatherin' firewood. And Willie's dead. So it looks like you're going to have to believe my story whether you want to or not."

Dolan repeated his question, "How many feet away, Cal?"

"Why come to think of it, I guess it must have been six or eight feet away from him. I guess I figured at the time that Willie had staggered back when Aragon shot him in the head."

Dolan said, "If Aragon put that gun where Willie could make a try at getting his hands on it and then shot him when he did, it's premeditated murder. Is that what you think happened, Cal?"

Again there was silence from Daybright as he carefully weighed what he would say. Once more Aragon took advantage of his silence to defend himself. "What the hell are you trying to do to me? I didn't murder Willie, I shot him in self-defense while he was trying to escape."

"How? He wasn't strong enough to get up on a horse."

"You wouldn't say that if you'd seen him. He had that rifle, and he was goin' for that horse like he wasn't no more'n just a little lame."

Daybright shook his head. "He's lying, Mr. Dolan. He's got to be lying. When I left to gather firewood, Willie's eyes were closed. His face was pale, and he was hardly breathin', seemed like. He sure as hell

couldn't have tried to escape less than five minutes afterward. And even if he had, Aragon could have
stopped him without killin' him. No, sir. If Willie
had a gun and was out of that travois, it was because
Aragon put the gun where he couldn't help but get
his hands on it."

"Will you swear to that in court?"

Daybright hesitated but only briefly. Then he said,
"Yes, sir, I sure will. That boy was murdered, just as
sure as I'm standing here."

Dolan glanced toward Aragon. It was now so dark
that he couldn't see the marshal's face. He said,
"When we get back, Aragon, I'm going to charge you
with the murder of Willie Brundage."

"You'll never make it stick."

"Maybe not. But even if you get off, you'll lose
your marshal's job."

There was silence for several moments after that.
Aragon's breathing was audible, harshly sighing in
and out. He turned away. His voice was only a sullen
growl. "*If* we get back, you bastard. *If* we get back."

Dolan replied evenly, "We'll get back, Aragon.
Some of us will. If you don't make it, it'll be your
own damn fault."

If there had been any doubt in him before about
Aragon's intent to kill him, it no longer remained.
From now on, he would have to watch Aragon every
minute of every day. Only by doing so could he hope
to stay alive.

CHAPTER FOURTEEN

W HEN THE FIRE had died to a bed of coals, Dolan
got bacon from his sack and put it in a skillet to
cook. Flora had flour and salt in her store of provisions, and Dolan mixed up biscuits to fry in the
bacon grease. The food smelled good, but even
though dark had fallen, the heat did not abate. Dolan supposed that by midnight it might begin to cool
off a bit. Until then it would continue to be oppressive and uncomfortable.

Aragon had built another fire, not far from the one
Sam Joseph had built earlier. Now he and Grogan
and Sims squatted around it, cooking their own food,
boiling their own coffee. That suited Dolan fine. He
liked none of the three and wanted as little to do
with them as possible.

Occasionally he glanced at Flora's face in the firelight. It was dusty and sunburned and tired, but there
was a serenity about it that he found attractive.
Twice she felt his glance and looked at him. Both
times she smiled.

Sam Joseph squatted across the fire, his sweating
black face catching highlights from it. He didn't look
at Aragon. Dolan wondered what kind of thoughts
were going around in his head. He knew that Sam
wouldn't forgive Aragon for the names he had used

on him or for his contempt. He felt a sudden kinship
with Sam and realized that Sam's hatred of Aragon
might be important to all of them before they got
back to town.

They finished eating, and the coals of the fire either died or became covered with gray ash that hid
their light. Dolan said, "Morning comes early," and
got up to get his blankets from behind the saddle he
had borrowed from Dunklee. He paid no attention to
the others except to say, "Sam, why don't you take
the first watch? Call me in three hours and I'll take
the second one."

Sam didn't reply. The others moved about in
darkness, spreading their blankets, getting ready to
sleep. Dolan couldn't distinguish their shapes in the
darkness, but he suddenly wondered where Flora was.
Softly he called, "Mrs. Doniphan? Where are you?"

There was no reply. A little louder, he called,
"Mrs. Doniphan!"

There still was no reply. Concerned now, Dolan
called, "Floyd?"

There was no answer from Aragon. Dolan cursed
angrily beneath his breath. He might have expected
this. Flora had probably moved away from the group
in the darkness for some needed privacy, and Aragon
had followed her.

The worst of it was, he had no idea which way they
might have gone. He held himself still, listening for
Flora's voice, listening for sounds of a struggle. The
others continued their preparations for retiring until
Dolan said sharply, "Quiet!"

For several moments the camp was utterly silent.
Dolan thought he heard a sound and cocked his head
in that direction, intently listening. He heard it
again, a sound like one that someone might make
crashing against a clump of brush.

There was quiet fury in him as he headed through

the darkness toward the sound. Aragon was nothing more nor less than a predatory animal. He took what he wanted, regardless of law or consequences. He killed when it served his purposes, raped when he felt desire, stole when he saw something he wanted for himself. He supposed he should have warned Flora about leaving camp, mainly because of the skulking Indians, but he hadn't thought of it.

He moved slowly and quietly, listening, trying to avoid crashing into clumps of brush or stumbling. Once more, ahead, he heard the sound of breaking brush and heard another sound like a single grunt of violent exertion.

Why didn't she cry out, he asked himself. Had Aragon already knocked her out? He broke into a run, his anger mounting at the thought.

He could now hear other sounds ahead. There was more grunts of exertion, mingled with an occasional breathless curse or muttered obscenity. And there were sounds like those someone might make if their mouth and nose were muffled by a hand or by some kind of cloth tied over them.

Dolan yelled, "Aragon!" but he didn't slow his pace. And suddenly he saw two struggling figures head of him, blurred and indistinct because of the almost complete darkness.

Briefly and fleetingly he wished he had brought Sam Joseph along with him to keep watch for the Ute renegades, but it was too late now to worry about that. He charged the struggling pair, distinguishing Flora from Aragon at the last moment. He reached out and hooked a forearm around Aragon's neck, tightening it with savage pleasure until he heard the man choke and gasp for air.

Aragon's grasp on Flora Doniphan loosened, and she broke away. She had one of Aragon's blankets thrown over her head. She fought free of it, her breath coming fast and hard, but neither screaming nor crying out. Dolan said harshly, "Damn you, Aragon, I ought to break your neck!"

Aragon was fighing now, fighting desperately for air. Dolan tightened his forearm, denying Aragon a single breath. He said between his teeth. "Can you find your way back to camp, Mrs. Doniphan?"

"I . . . I'm afraid not. I don't know which way . . ."

"Then stay right where you are. Don't go wandering off. Those Utes might still be around someplace."

He knew what he was going to do, even as he spoke to her. He'd had his fill of Aragon. He didn't know how badly Aragon had hurt her or even if he had hurt her at all. But he did know that Aragon had intended raping her when he followed her from camp. He released the marshal suddenly, giving him a savage push that sent him reeling away for a dozen feet.

Aragon turned, still choking for air, but having enough breath to gasp, "What the hell's the matter with you, Dolan? You know what she is!"

The words turned Dolan's fury into something cold, more deadly than any heat of anger could ever be. He said softly, "Aragon, this is something I've been promising myself ever since we left. Don't try to talk me out of it."

He took a step toward Aragon, another and another still. There was a primitive kind of pleasure in him now. He *had* been looking forward to a showdown with Aragon, however he had tried to avoid it in the interests of catching up with the outlaws who had robbed the bank. But there was no use trying to avoid it now. No time would be lost by his fighting the marshal here tonight.

He supposed Aragon would go for his gun and try killing him. He suddenly discovered he didn't care. If

Aragon pulled his gun, he'd take it away from him and jam it down his throat until he choked on it.

A report roared ahead and flame stabbed toward him. The bullet seared along his ribs, burning, bringing blood. He said, "Ah! I hoped you'd do that, Aragon, because it gives me all the excuse I need for doing what I want to do."

He plunged forward, flinging himself at Aragon's lower body to avoid the marshal's second shot. It roared immediately above his head, and then his body struck Aragon's and the marshal was flung backward into a spiny greasewood clump.

Dolan had locked his arms around Aragon's legs. The marshal tried clubbing him with the gun. He released the man and clawed for possession of the gun.

Aragon was younger than he, and his body was strong and powerful in spite of its paunchiness. But a rage burned in Dolan that would not be denied. He clawed along the ground until he reached the gun, hardly feeling the two grazing blows that Aragon struck with it. He yanked the gun out of Aragon's stubby hand as though Aragon had been a child, and in his fury flung it a hundred feet away into the brush.

Aragon bawled, "Sims! Grogan!" and Dolan smashed his fist into the burly marshal's mouth, which immediately began to babble obscenities. Dolan smashed the marshal's mouth again, growling, "Shut up! Shut your filthy mouth!"

Flora Doniphan stood frozen, motionless, a dozen feet away. Her clothes were torn, but she seemed unaware of it.

Aragon's powerful body convulsed, and he managed to throw Dolan back. He came up, his arms raised, both fists clenched, then came down on Dolan pounding with both fists at once. One struck Dolan's nose, and he could feel blood spurt from it. The other struck his shoulder where it joined his neck. The pain of that blow was so intense that for a moment he thought he was paralyzed.

He half rolled, doubled his body, then straightened, kicking Aragon in the chest with both feet at once. Wind drove out of the man with an explosive, gusty sound, and afterward he gasped helplessly there on his back, trying to fill his lungs again. Dolan got to his feet. Aragon came up, still gasping, and Dolan swung a long, looping right at him, aiming for his head, shadowy because of the utter darkness in which they fought.

The blow struck Aragon in the eye with a shock that Dolan felt all the way to his shoulder. Aragon went back, bawling again, "Sims! Grogan!"

Dolan heard running feet. He swung his head gleefully. Now was a good time to clean out all the dissidents, he thought, and yelled, "Come on, Sims! Come on, Grogan! Come get your goddam feet wet if you've got the stomach for it!"

He could hear his own voice roaring as if it came from far away. He could never recall having been this furious in all his life. Aragon struggled to his feet, a rock almost as big as his head in both his hands. Flora Doniphan screamed, "Look out! Look out!"

Webb Dolan swung his head to look at Aragon again. The running feet were closer, crashing through brush they failed to avoid in the dark. He saw Aragon, the rock held above his head, staggering toward him. The rock came forward and began its descent toward his head. . . .

Desperately, he flung himself aside. He didn't even think about his gun, still in its holster at his side. He didn't think about it because he didn't want to end this fight. He had just begun, and he wasn't through with Aragon. When he was, Aragon would lie bleeding on the ground, unable to move, speak or raise his head. For three days now he had tolerated Aragon's rebelliousness, arrogance, threats and abuse. Tonight he was fighting back.

The rock grazed his head as it descended. Aragon let it go, and it rolled away harmlessly into the brush. Dolan wildly swung his fists, feeling them connect, feeling them sink into Aragon's flabby paunch. Gusts of wind drove out of Aragon as they struck, and he staggered back, overwhelmed by Dolan's ferocity. Once more he cried out frantically, "Grogan! Sims! For God's sake. . . ."

Dolan backed him against a tall, spiny greasewood clump that was higher than his head. Aragon fell back into it, fighting its yielding bulk and trying to push himself forward and upright again but failing because of Dolan's pounding fists. His nose smashed, and after that his mouth. He spit teeth helplessly as Dolan's fists continued to lacerate him and drive him back deeper into the yielding greasewood clump.

Grogan and Sims came running and Flora Doniphan cried out and Dolan turned like a wolf at bay. Behind him, Aragon struggled helplessly with the greasewood clump, only burying himself deeper in it the more he struggled to escape.

Dolan stepped aside as the first shadowy figure charged recklessly at him. He brought both hands, clasped, down on the back of the man's neck and watched him pitch forward and lie completely still. Immediately behind, the second man, slighter than the first and therefore Sims, stopped as suddenly as if he had run headlong into a wall. Dolan said softly, "Come on, come on. Come and get your share."

Sims turned and hurried back toward camp. By now, Aragon had managed to free himself from the clawing brush. He tried to slip away, but Dolan overtook him and dragged him back. "Huh uh. You can't quit. You're in this to the bitter end."

Desperately, Aragon wrestled him, trying now for the gun in its holster at Dolan's side. Dolan brought a savage punch into the marshal's stomach. Aragon gasped for breath. He doubled, clutching himself, as he fought for air.

Dolan became aware of Flora's voice. "Sheriff! Mr. Dolan, please! That's enough. You'll kill him if you don't stop!"

Dazedly, Dolan swung his head to look at her. She was only a shadowy shape a dozen feet away. He swung back to Aragon.

Spread-legged, suddenly a little dizzy himself, he brought back his right fist as far as it would go, then threw it forward with every bit of his body weight in back of it.

It struck Aragon squarely in the middle of his face, flinging him back half a dozen feet. Aragon lay completely still.

Panting, Dolan straightened with difficulty. His hand felt as if he had broken it, but he discovered he could open and close it without too much pain. He said hoarsely, "Ma'am, I'll escort you back to camp."

The sound she made was more unexpected than anything that had happened yet. She giggled. She giggled and then began to laugh.

Dolan stared blankly toward her for a moment, completely taken by surprise. Then a grin spread across his face. He chuckled breathlessly.

She took his arm, and they staggered back toward camp, stumbling over rocks and low clumps of brush. Only when they reached the others, waiting silently in camp, did their laughing stop. Suddenly it seemed as ridiculous as the things that had prompted it. Dolan sank down weakly onto the ground and began struggling to pull off his boots. After he had done so, he looked at his side where Aragon's bullet had grazed his ribs. It would be sore, but the wound wasn't even deep enough to need bandaging. So far his luck had held.

CHAPTER FIFTEEN

DOLAN HEARD SIMS and Grogan talking sympathetically to Aragon as they helped him back into camp half an hour later. Aragon wasn't saying anything. He had not, apparently, been able to find his gun. He and the others settled down in their blankets. Dolan noted in his mind where they put their beds, but once they settled down, they did not move again. At midnight, when Sam Joseph called him, he got up and took over the watch. Dolan didn't intend to let the camp be surprised by the skulking Utes. Nor did he want Aragon sneaking up on him while he was asleep.

It was still dark when he shook Sam Joseph awake. Sam sat up and pulled on his boots. He buckled his gun belt around his waist. Sam moved around the camp, calling each of the posse members, leaving Flora Doniphan for Dolan to awaken because he was afraid he might frighten her. When he had awakened everyone, he stirred the remains of last night's fire, added wood and put some water for coffee into a pan and set it on to heat.

Dolan groped through the darkness to where the horses were picketed. He led them into camp, saddled and bridled his own and Flora Doniphan's. She was up, now, busy at the fire preparing breakfast for the men.

Aragon's nose had swelled to almost double its former size. Both his eyes were black. His mouth had also swelled and his lips were split. Dolan stared at him with grim satisfaction.

The air was not cool, but it wasn't nearly as hot as it had been yesterday. The men ate quickly and silently, almost sullenly, Dolan thought. Daybright approached him as he moved away from the fire. The man seemed troubled and hesitant. Dolan asked, "What's the matter with you?"

Cal Daybright shrugged. "Damned if I know, Webb. Hunch, maybe."

"Hunch about what?"

"About this posse, I suppose. About going on."

"You're not suggesting that we give up and go back?"

Cal Daybright shrugged again. "I don't know. Maybe I am."

"For God's sake, why? What about Susan? What about those two ahead of us who ran her down?"

"Killing them isn't going to bring her back."

"I'm not going to kill them. I'm going to take them alive."

"You don't know that. You can't be sure. How do you know Aragon won't murder them?"

"Well, I don't know. But I'm going to keep a damn close watch."

"But . . ."

Dolan said impatiently, "They knew the chance they took when they robbed the bank."

"Did Willie Brundage know what kind of chance he took?"

"We're not talking about him. We're talking about the other two. And about the eight thousand dollars that belongs to the people of Pagosa and the surrounding area. If we don't get it back, the bank will probably go broke. Have you any idea how many people get hurt when a bank goes broke?"

Daybright nodded miserably. "I know. I guess this hunch has got under my hide. I've got a feeling that if we go on, none of us will be coming back."

"You're just upset about Willie."

"Maybe that's it. But Aragon knows that if he goes back, he'll have to stand trial for murder. He knows you'll arrest him and that I'll be a witness against him. What would be simpler for him than just killing us?"

Dolan stared at him soberly. The sky was gray now with coming day. A few desert birds were chirping, heralding the dawn. Dolan said, "I can't go back. I'm sworn to go on as long as I'm able to."

"Then let me go back."

Dolan hesitated. Then he shook his head. "I can't do that either. I need you. You and Sam are the only two that I can trust. Besides, I wouldn't let anyone go back alone. The Utes would jump him, and that would be the end of that."

"I'm willing to take the chance." Daybright's face was still pleading, but no longer did he show much hope.

Again Dolan shook his head. "I'm sorry."

"You can't keep me against my will."

"Maybe not. But I can charge you when we get back. I can see that you go to trial."

Daybright stared at him exasperatedly. "Damn it, Webb, I don't want to run out on you. I'd just like to talk some sense into your damn stubborn head!"

Dolan grinned unexpectedly. "You're just wasting your time. It's been tried before."

He glanced around and saw that the others were almost ready to leave. He led Flora's horse to her and helped her mount. Her face was drawn and tired and there was the slightest of worried frowns upon her brow, but she smiled at him as he helped her up.

He nodded shortly at Sam, who took the trail at a steady trot. Dolan looked at Aragon. "You're next. Stay ahead of me. I want to keep an eye on you."

Aragon scowled, then winced with the pain the grimace caused. He reined his horse after the tracker and kicked him into a trot. Dolan followed, beckoning Flora to fall in just behind. Daybright rode behind Flora. Sims and Grogan brought up the rear.

There was irritation in Dolan today because he hadn't managed the posse better than he had. Too many things had been going wrong. For an instant he wondered if Daybright might not be right. Maybe they should return. Maybe their lives were more valuable than capturing two outlaws and recovering the money stolen from the bank. The trouble was, Aragon and Sims and Grogan wouldn't go back even if he and the others did. They'd go on, kill the outlaws and get the money for themselves.

He turned his head and surprised Flora Doniphan studying him. She flushed when he caught her eye. He found himself wishing that he could take Daybright and Sam and Flora and just turn around. Even if the lives of the men weren't important enough, Flora's was. He suddenly became aware that he was staring at her steadily. Her flush had deepened painfully. He quickly looked away.

Thinking about giving up was ridiculous, he thought. He'd been a lawman for more years than he cared to count. Duty was as much a part of him as his arms or legs. It was his duty to capture the outlaws and recover the stolen money if he could. And that was what he was going to do.

The sun came up behind them, uncomfortably hot the instant its rays touched their backs. Ahead, there was not a cloud in the sky. There was only the desert, scarred by arroyos and ravines, its monotony occasionally broken by a rising, rocky butte.

Dust raised from the hooves of the two horses ahead of him. It was a grayish-yellow dust that coated Dolan's horse, coated his legs and arms, that filled his lungs and occasionally made him cough.

In midmorning they reached another water hole. It had been deliberately muddied, just as the first one had. Dolan looked at Sam Joseph. "Looks like they know this desert pretty well."

Sam nodded. "They know what they're doin', Mr. Dolan. But I know what I'm doin', too."

"How far are they ahead of us?"

"I make it seven hours now. They ain't hurryin' like they was. They figure they goin' to make us drop back by muddyin' these water holes."

"Won't they?"

"If we drop back, we'll lose them outlaws, Mr. Dolan. We'll lose them for good."

Dolan nodded. The horses might give out before they caught the two bank robbers, but if they didn't push on and keep pushing, they'd lose the outlaws anyway.

Now the horses sucked noisily at the thin film of unmuddied water on the surface of the water hole. Long before they'd had their fill, the clear water was gone and the riders had to pull them away.

They went on, heading west. And now, as the heat increased, it was plain that Aragon's lacerated face had begun to hurt him even more.

Dolan turned in his saddle and looked behind. Flora Doniphan rode almost numbly, her head drooping forward. Behind her, Daybright was squinting against the merciless glare of the desert sun, reflected up from the rocks and gray-white soil. His face was flushed, as were the faces of Sims and Grogan, just behind.

Both Sims and Grogan looked edgy and irritable. They met Dolan's stare and scowled before they looked away.

Ahead, Aragon rode in a strangely hunched position, as though favoring muscles that were sore. He also seemed irritable. Only Sam Joseph was his usual, imperturbable self. His black face shone with sweat. His eyes were calm, his expression intent. He was lucky in that he had something to keep his mind occupied, Dolan thought. Following the trail took all his concentration because wind had, in places, all but erased the outlaws' tracks.

Dolan halted them at noon. They dismounted and fanned the horses' backs with the saddle blankets that now stank of stale horse sweat. There was little shade for the men and for Flora Doniphan. There was none for the horses.

Dolan kept them there, hunched beneath the scrub greasewood bushes for half an hour. Then he signaled them to saddle up and mount.

Once more they headed out. Behind them, the rising escarpment of the Ute Plateau was shrouded with desert haze. Dolan wondered where the Indians were and if they still were following. He began to watch the horizon intently to right and left and at last was rewarded by the sight of a thin wisp of dust rising on the right. He called, "Sam," and pointed toward the dust.

Sam squinted, watching the dust disappear, then reappear, then disappear again. He looked at Dolan finally. "Them Indians, Mr. Dolan. They ain't much more'n a mile away."

Dolan glanced behind at Daybright, suddenly assailed by the same premonition that had previously bothered the storekeeper. Daybright was frowning, staring toward the dust raised by the Indians. Dolan glanced away, impatient with himself. He was getting to be an old woman, letting Daybright's fearful hunches become his own.

But the premonition did not go away. It stayed all through the long, dragging afternoon.

Near four o'clock, Dolan saw a distant curtain of dust ahead. Sam also noticed it. He began hurrying toward a shallow bluff ahead and slightly to the left. Dolan didn't say anything to the others, but he knew what the dust curtain was. It was a sandstorm, less than a dozen miles away, approaching at frightening speed. He wondered if they would reach the bluff before the sandstorm enveloped them.

Sam Joseph suddenly kicked his horse into a lope. He pointed to the approaching yellow cloud. "Sandstorm! We'll have to try and reach that bluff."

Dolan held back until Aragon had spurred his horse after Sam. He was damned if he was going to let Aragon drop back now. He also let Flora Doniphan ride on ahead, and Daybright and the other two. Then he followed, watching the rolling clouds of air-borne sand.

The bluff was now less than half a mile away, the sandstorm no more than five. With luck, they'd reach it, Dolan thought. But if the sandstorm enveloped them before they did, they'd have no choice but to stop and dismount and wait it out wherever it caught up with them.

Sam Joseph also saw how close it was going to be. He raked his horse's side, repeatedly with his spurs, forcing the overheated weary animal to run.

The posse thundered toward the bluff, reached it and dismounted, just as the first blast of wind and sand struck, howling, blinding, so thick it obliterated the sun and turned daylight into dusk.

CHAPTER SIXTEEN

STUNG BY THE driving sand, nearly blinded by the first blast of it, Dolan knuckled his eyes with one hand and hung on desperately to the reins with the other. The horse pulled back, wanting not to get his rump to the wind, to drift with it, his being an instinctive urge as old as time itself. Dolan could see shadowy shapes ahead, horses and people, and he fought on toward the doubtful shelter of the bluff. The sandstorm was roaring in diagonally to the bluff, so that full protection from its merciless blast was impossible.

He shouted, "Flora!" and listened, and when he thought he heard her voice cry out, he hurried that way, fearful that her horse might get away from her and be lost in the driving sand before anybody could do anything.

He was not unaware of the possibility that Aragon would choose this opportunity to try killing him. He was further aware that Aragon might try disarming him and Sam Joseph and Daybright, too.

He bumped into a horse, and the animal shied away, snorting and kicking out at him, but he went on and suddenly slammed into Flora, nearly knocking her off her feet. Just in time, he seized her horse's reins. Holding both horses now, he pushed Flora toward the sloping side of the bluff, wishing it could have been a vertical rock escarpment instead of only sloping earth. He yelled, "Sit down and put your back to the wind! Pull something over your face, and breath through it! It'll sift out some of the sand and dust!"

She collapsed, drawing up her knees, bending forward to put her face down into her skirt. Dolan sank down on the windward side of her, still knuckling the dust out of his burning, streaming eyes, still clinging desperately to the two horses' reins.

It was now almost dark, as driving sand blotted out the sun. Wind made a sighing, whistling sound coming over the bluff and down to meet the resistance of people and horses on the lee side of it. The few stunted clumps of brush whipped back and forth in the tremendous wind. Sand, striking bodies and saddles, made a low roar that was unique and unmistakable.

Beside him Flora Doniphan sat, hugging her knees against her, face buried in the folds of her dress. Her hair, now gray with accumulated sand, whipped out and grew tangled in the wind.

Dolan's hat nearly sailed off his head. He crammed it down tighter. The horses were pulling against the reins, fighting to get their rumps to the savage ferocity of driving sand. Dolan hung on tenaciously, wrapping the reins of both horses around his wrist as further insurance against letting go. If they bolted, they'd drag him with them, although he could always save himself by letting go. He tried not to think about being stranded out here with no food, water or horses. He tried not to think of the consequences if the horses did manage to get away. They'd drift for miles, their trail obliterated by the wind. . . .

Suddenly he realized that the outlaws' trail had

also been obliterated. The wind would, by now, have scoured the desert clean.

No use worrying about that. Choking, eyes streaming even though they now were tightly shut, he hunched forward, trying to ignore the sting of sand, covering his nose and mouth with his free hand in which he clutched a bandana handkerchief.

He felt Flora move closer until their bodies touched. He could feel her warmth, her trembling. He felt a sudden compassion for her. The last couple of days had been terrible ones for her. Enough things had happened to her to demoralize anyone. Her husband had been murdered before her eyes. She had been attacked by Aragon and frightened by the knowledge that the Utes were after her. Now this must also be endured.

She raised her head long enough to shriek at him, "How long do these storms last?"

"It may last the rest of the day! The winds usually quiet down when it begins to get dark!"

She nodded dumbly and put her face down into her skirt again. Dolan's skin felt as if it was cracking in the dry, overheated wind. He licked his lips and tasted grit. He closed his eyes again, knowing they were red and rimmed with mud.

Now it became a thing to be borne, to be waited out as patiently as possible. The horses still tugged at the reins occasionally, but most of the time they seemed to have accepted the fact that they could not get away. A couple of times Dolan opened his eyes and glanced away toward his right. He could see blurred shapes through the gloom and driving sand, but he could not recognize anyone.

Aragon must be in torment, he thought. Sand and dirt blowing into the lacerations on his face must be excruciatingly painful.

For what seemed hours, the wind continued, unabated. But gradually it grew less ferocious, the dust clouds whipping past less thick. The sun became visible as a dim, luminous ball in the western sky.

Dolan fumbled for his watch, drew it out and looked at it. It was not quite six o'colck. They had been in the dust storm less than two hours. But it had seemed like more.

He waited another ten minutes. In that time, the dust began to settle out of the air and the wind died to a stiff breeze not strong enough to lift more dust from the ground. He got stiffly to his feet.

Flora struggled to rise, and he reached down and helped her up. Sam Joseph, his black face gray with dust, approached, leading his horse. Dolan said, "See if there's anything left of the trail."

"No use, Mr. Dolan. That there trail's gone." "We'll try finding it anyhow."

"No use, Mr. Dolan. I know what I'm talkin' about."

"You think those bank robbers might have been caught in the same sandstorm?"

Sam shrugged. "Depends on how big it was."

"Do you think you can pick up their trail farther on?"

The tracker looked doubtful. "Ain't much chance."

"What then? Have you got any idea what they might be headed for?"

"I got an idea, but it could be wrong."

"What is it?"

"They been pointin' straight toward McGuffy's Trading Post. The trouble is, that don't mean they goin' there. Mebbe they just want us to think they are."

"They couldn't have known this sandstorm would wipe out their trail."

Sam agreed, "No. But sandstorms they pretty common down here this time of year."

"How far is McGuffy's Trading Post?"

Sam frowned as though trying to remember exact distances. At last he said, "Ain't been there but once, so I ain't real sure. Eight, ten hours mebbe."

Dolan began to pace nervously back and forth. He glanced at Flora, who was trying to comb some of the grit out of her hair and fighting the tangles the wind had put into it. He glanced at Aragon, hunched miserably on the ground, staring blankly ahead of him. Sims and Grogan stood nearby, numb and passive. Daybright was wiping dust from his face with a grimy bandanna handkerchief.

He knew the horses needed water desperately. He knew how tired they were. Another day of heat and sun might exhaust the horses and sap the will of the posse members. They might well refuse to go on after that.

But if they rested now until an hour after dark . . . if they went on in darkness, there would be neither heat nor sun to make the horses' thirst unbearable and further exhaust the men.

He looked at Sam. "Think you could find McGuffy's in the dark?"

Sam grinned. "I can find it."

"All right. We'll rest here until an hour after dark and then go on. Maybe we can end this chase tonight." He crossed to Aragon's horse and removed the marshal's rifle from the saddle boot. He didn't want the two outlaws warned again.

He called, "We'll rest here until after dark! We'll have coffee and some food. Use a little water to wash the dust out of your horses' nostrils. Use a little to wash your faces if you want. But keep a little, too. I think we'll find water before daylight, but I can't be sure."

Sam was already moving around, gathering small sticks of dead brush to make the fire with. Flora

hastily repinned her hair, then began to make
preparations for the meal. Dolan watched her admir-
ingly. She was dead tired, and she was certainly saddlesore. But she had not complained and she had not
shirked. Doniphan had been a fool, he thought. If he
hadn't been able to forget her past, to take her as she
was, he had been the world's worst fool.

The fire crackled in the oppressive heat. A pan
filled with bacon began to sizzle. Coffee began to boil,
filling the air with its aroma.

Dolan smiled at Flora and she smiled back. For the
moment, his premonition of disaster faded. He got his
cup and poured it half-full of coffee. He sipped it,
thinking that never in his life had coffee tasted quite
this good. The others shuffled to the fire like sleep-
walkers, still stunned by the fury of the storm. Dolan
could see that they now had little hope of catching
the outlaw pair.

He himself knew that McGuffy's Trading Post was
the last chance he was going to get. If he didn't catch
the outlaws there, he would have to give up and go
back to town.

Sims and Grogan stuck close to Aragon. Sometimes
they talked in low tones that no one else could hear,
but mostly they were glumly silent. Daybright took
his plate and cup to the side of the bluff and squatted
there to eat. Aragon squatted down next to him.

Aragon was obviously as stunned as anyone. But
there was a brooding fury in him, too. Occasionally
he would raise a grimy bandanna to his face to blot
at one of the lacerations made by Dolan's fists. Each
time he did, he would wince, then look at Dolan balefully. It was as if he were making some kind of
promise to himself. A couple of times he growled
something at Daybright, sitting at his side.

Daybright finished eating and scoured his plate
with sand. He crossed to Dolan. His face, like those of

the others, was covered with a layer of grayish dust. His eyes were rimmed with mud formed by a mixture of dust and tears. His lips were dry and cracked, and now he licked them uncomfortably. He asked, "What are we going to do? Are we going back? We've lost the trail, haven't we?"

Dolan nodded. "We've lost the trail."

"Are we going back?"

Dolan shook his head. "There's one more thing I want to try. If that fails, then we'll go back."

"What's that?"

"Sam Joseph says there's a trading post maybe eight or ten hours away. McGuffy's Trading Post. He says the trail was pointing straight at it, so there's a good chance that the outlaws have gone there. They need fresh horses as much as we do. But if we don't catch them there, then we'll go back."

Daybright nodded. He said, "A man's a funny critter, Webb. When we left Pagosa, I couldn't wait to get them in my sights. If we'd caught them the first day, I'd have killed all three without feeling anything. But after we caught that wounded boy . . . well, I guess I began to change. He was only a boy, and he hadn't meant to do anything wrong. And he was so sorry about running Susan down. . . ."

Dolan said, "A man cools off with time." He glanced at Aragon and wondered if the marshal was ever going to cool off. He doubted it. Aragon was the kind that would brood and hate until he did something about his hate. In this case, doing something meant killing. He was glad that Aragon was no longer armed. For an instant he considered disarming both Sims and Grogan to keep them from sharing their guns with Aragon, but he decided it was impractical. If he disarmed Grogan and Sims, there would be only three armed men against the outlaws, and that wouldn't be enough.

He called, "All of you lie down and try to get some
sleep. We're going to be traveling all night, and you'll
need all the rest that you can get. Unsaddle the
horses first and fan their backs. Then picket them."

Grogan yelled, "Where are you going, for God's
sake? The trail's wiped out."

"McGuffy's Trading Post. Sam thinks that's where
they went."

"And what if they ain't there?"

"Then we'll have to give it up. Unless we'd just
happen to be lucky enough to pick up their trail. In
a thousand square miles of desert, it ain't very likely,
I can tell you that."

There was some grumbling from Grogan, Sims and
Aragon, but the three unsaddled their horses and
fanned their sweating backs. They picketed the horses
and lay down not far away. For a while they talked in
low tones among themselves, but eventually they qui-
eted and lay still.

Dolan unsaddled his own and Flora's horse. He
fanned their backs while she scoured the blackened
cooking utensils clean with sand. He led the horses to
where Aragon and his two cronies had picketed theirs
and staked them out.

Flora had stretched out on the far side of the little
camp. Her eyes were closed.

Dolan laid down and pillowed his head on his
saddle. His own rifle was in the saddle boot. Aragon's
hung from the saddle horn by a thong.

His eyes burned fiercely when he closed them. He
felt jumpy and nervous, but at least he slept, a
restless, uneasy sleep in which he dreamed he was
being stalked. The dream was even more uneasy and
disturbing because he couldn't find out who was
stalking him.

CHAPTER SEVENTEEN

DOLAN AWAKENED SUDDENLY. He sat upright and stared into the darkness toward the sounds that had awakened him. They weren't hard to identify. They were those of horses galloping.

He snatched his rifle out of the saddle boot, levered a cartridge into the chamber and leaped to his feet. His mind was still dazed with sleep, and all he could think was, "Indians." He hadn't posted a guard tonight for the first time since they'd left town. He'd thought everyone needed all the rest they could get, and he'd been sure the Indians would have lost their trail just as they had lost the outlaws' trail.

He yelled, "Sam! Daybright!" already running toward the sounds of receding hoofs. And then he knew. The hoofbeats hadn't been made by the ponies of the six Ute renegades. They had been made by the posse's horses. By all of them. The area where they had been picketed was empty. He and Sam and Daybright and Flora Doniphan were stranded out here without horses. They were afoot thirty miles from anywhere.

Sam Joseph came up at his side silently. He said fatalistically, "Well, it looks like he finally got even with you, Mr. Dolan."

Daybright asked excitedly, "Where are the horses? Was that our horses I heard? Who . . ."

Dolan said, "Aragon. He and Grogan and Sims left and took all the horses along with them."

"For God's sake, why . . .?"

"They figure on catching the outlaws and getting the bank's money for themselves. Whether they do or don't, I doubt if we'll ever see any of them again."

"What about us? My God, Webb, we're stranded out here. We haven't got enough water to last half a day."

It was now well after dark, but the heat was still oppressive. No breeze stirred. Sand still hung suspended in the air.

Dolan was raging inwardly, calling Aragon every name he knew. He wished he had killed the marshal when he'd had the chance. He wished he had beaten him so badly that he couldn't travel at all. Most of all, he wished he had refused to let Aragon come along in the first place. He might not have been able to make the refusal stick, but he could have tried.

Flora had been awakened by the commotion and now was standing at his side. He turned his head.

She asked, "What are we going to do?"

"Walk. That's all we *can* do."

Daybright's voice had risen. "We can't walk out of here! We're about played out as it is, and Sam said it was six or eight hours to McGuffy's on horseback."

Dolan asked dryly, "You got any better ideas?"

"You should have posted a guard! Then it couldn't have happened. You've had a guard every other night. Why didn't you have one tonight?"

"I didn't think it was necessary. I figured the Utes had lost our trail in the sandstorm."

"You might have known Aragon would try something like this. You knew he was figuring on going after that money for himself."

Sam said, "Blame ain't goin' to get us nowhere, Mr. Daybright. Don't matter who's to blame. We're here afoot an' that's that."

Daybright said accusingly, "With practically no food or water. We can't make it, I tell you! What if we can't find McGuffy's Trading Post?"

Dolan said, "All right, Mr. Daybright. We're in a fix. Nobody says we're not. But it's not going to do a bit of good to get worked up. The thing to do is get started walking now. Standing here arguing isn't going to help a bit."

Daybright grumbled something he didn't hear. He said, "Get what you need off your saddles. Food and water. Guns and ammunition. Leave everything else."

He had a hunch that the next time he saw the saddles it would be on the backs of the Ute renegades' ponies. He gave Aragon's rifle to Flora. "Carry that. If you get tired, I'll carry it. I don't want to leave it behind for the Indians."

She accepted the rifle. It was too dark to see her face, but he could tell she was trembling. He said reassuringly, "Don't worry. We'll make it."

She did not reply. Sam Joseph led out, guiding himself, Dolan supposed by the stars. He waited until Flora followed, then he fell in behind her. Daybright brought up the rear.

For a while they walked in silence, each thinking his own gloomy thoughts. Dolan's were concerned, firstly, with whether Sam Joseph was going to be able to find McGuffy's Trading Post. Guiding himself by the stars instead of by landmarks was bound to be risky. He might miss it altogether, and if that happened, then the four of them were sure to die of thirst, hunger, exhaustion or a combination of the three.

His second worry was the Indians. Come dawn, they were sure to find the posse's camp and the abandoned saddles. When they did, they would know that four members of the posse, including the woman they coveted, were afoot. They'd overtake the four easily. Unless he and the others were lucky enough to find cover when the Utes caught up, they wouldn't have a chance.

His third worry was the most serious. He knew they might arrive at McGuffy's to find it burned to the ground, to find McGuffy dead. Aragon wasn't likely to leave a potential witness against him alive, and McGuffy would have been witness to the murder of the outlaws and the seizure of the stolen money.

Following this reasoning further, Dolan realized that if Aragon and his two followers killed McGuffy, then they'd have to burn the trading post to conceal their crime. It would then be assumed that McGuffy had been killed by marauding Utes, and that would be the end of that.

In places the sand, piled up by the storm, was deep and soft, making it hard to walk. Sam Joseph plowed ahead tirelessly. Flora floundered after him, sometimes falling, but always getting up without complaint and going on again. Dolan caught up with her one of these times, helped her up and took Aragon's rifle away from her. "I'll carry that."

She resisted, trying to take the rifle back. "I can carry it for a while. I'll tell you when I can't."

Her voice was so firm that he gave the rifle back, faintly smiling to himself. Doniphan had, indeed, been a fool for not realizing what a jewel Flora was.

He tried to calculate how long it was going to take them to reach McGuffy's Trading Post on foot. If the horses could have made it in eight hours, it would take the four of them at least twice that long to make it afoot. Provided they made few stops. Provided the stops they did make were short.

But no matter how they tried, the stops were going

to become both more frequent and of longer duration. Flora was being brave, perhaps more so than Daybright was. But courage alone couldn't sustain her forever. Sooner or later she was going to give out, and he didn't dare leave her and go on. Not with the six Utes following.

It was probable, he admitted reluctantly, that Aragon had won. It was only a fifty-fifty chance that they'd ever reach McGuffy's alive.

On and on they plodded. Daybright, exhausted and out of breath, was no longer able to talk accusingly about who was to blame and about how poor their chances were. Dolan smiled faintly to himself, thinking what Daybright's reaction would be if he knew how slim their chances really were.

They had gone no more than a couple of miles when Flora collapsed to the ground. Dolan caught up and knelt beside her. She said, "I turned my ankle. I'll be all right in a minute."

Dolan called to Sam. "We'll have to stop for a few minutes, Sam."

Daybright now caught up, puffing and out of breath. Without speaking, he also sank down to the ground. Flora said, "I'm sorry."

"Nothing to be sorry for. You'll be all right in a minute, as soon as you catch your breath."

"I'm holding the rest of you back. You'll never catch those bank robbers unless you leave me behind."

"Nobody's going to leave anybody behind."

"You could leave Mr. Daybright with me. You and Mr. Joseph could go on, and after you've caught the bank robbers, you could come back."

"You really mean that, don't you? You'd really stay here and wait."

"Of course."

"Well, the answer's no. Those Utes are almost sure

to find our trail. They'd make quick work out of Day-bright and you."

She was silent a few moments. Then she said sheep-ishly, "I was hoping you'd say no. I guess I just had to offer to stay behind. I know how much it means to you—not only catching the bank robbers but catching Aragon."

He grinned in the darkness. "Catching Aragon is getting to be more important to me than catching the bank robbers and getting the money back."

"What do you think Aragon will do when he catches them? Is there a chance that he'll arrest them and bring them back?"

Dolan shrugged. "I don't think so, but maybe I'm being too hard on Aragon just because I don't like him."

"Then you think he'll take the money and go on?"

"Uh huh. After killing the bank robbers. And he'll probably have to kill McGuffy, too."

"And we haven't got a chance of getting there in time to keep it from happening."

"I'm afraid not."

She struggled to her feet. "I'm all right now."

He took Aragon's rifle from her, and this time she did not resist. Sam Joseph led out and Flora followed determinedly. Dolan let Daybright follow her because he didn't want Daybright falling behind the way Dunklee had a couple of days ago.

He was wearing high-heeled boots, and they didn't make walking any easier. In addition, all of them ex-cept Sam Joseph kept blundering into clumps of brush or stumbling over rocks and uneven places in the ground. The stars gave very little light.

Two more miles fell behind before they had to stop again. This time it was Daybright who halted them. He was breathing with a harshly rasping sound and complaining of pain in his chest and a numbness in his arm.

Dolan cursed silently, because he knew they were finished now. Daybright was in his late fifties at least. He might not have had trouble with his heart before, but he was having trouble now. If he was forced to go on, he would probably die because of it.

Flora knelt beside Daybright, more worried about him than about her own weariness. She took Dolan's canteen when he handed it to her and raised it to Daybright's mouth. Dolan said, "We'll rest an hour. Lie down, Cal, and try to get some sleep."

Daybright grunted something that Dolan did not understand. He lay down, though, still breathing harshly and heavily. Flora stayed beside him a few minutes, then got up and came to where Dolan was. "It's his heart, isn't it?"

"I'm afraid so."

"Does that mean we can't go on?"

"It means we're going to have to travel slower. It means that any chance we might have had of getting there in time is gone."

"Could you leave the three of us and go on yourself?"

"I could, but I'd probably miss the place."

"Then send Sam Joseph on."

He nodded. "That may be what I'll have to do. Somebody's got to get horses and bring them back to us."

She sat down and put her back to a rock. Dolan sat on the rock beside her where he could look down at her. Her face was only a blur in the faint starlight, but he didn't have to see it to remember what it was like. She said unexpectedly, "Tell me about yourself."

He was silent a moment, a bit startled at the abruptness of her words. Then he said, "There's not much excitement in my life and not many criminals to catch. Nowadays a sheriff serves legal papers—summonses and injunctions. Sometimes he has to make peace between two ranchers that are fighting over water rights or he has to break up a family quarrel. I like it, though. I guess I like people, and when I can, I like to help them out."

"And men like Aragon?"

"Well, there are good ones, and there are those like Aragon."

"You seem able to handle the ones like Aragon."

"I haven't done too well lately. I let him get away with the horses. I should have guessed he'd try. I guess I just didn't think he'd abandon us all out here to die."

"He knows Sam Joseph and he knows you. He knew the two of you wouldn't let us die."

He peered down at her, wishing he could see her face.

She was looking up at him. "That sounded like flattery, didn't it?"

He grinned faintly and nodded his head.

"Maybe it was. I want you to like me."

"I do like you. And I want to see you again after we get back."

"You'll change. You'll think about it and you'll change your mind. Just like Mr. Doniphan changed his." There was sudden and unexpected bitterness in her voice.

Dolan was silent a moment before he spoke. He sensed that he was on uncertain ground, and he wanted what he said to be just right. "I won't change. I guess I don't know how to convince you—not with words. But I won't change."

She didn't answer him. But the silence was companionable, and he knew she had accepted his words at face value. At least for now.

CHAPTER EIGHTEEN

Dolan laid back on the ground and stared up at the stars. He thought about the Utes, coming on behind. The Indians would catch up tomorrow, probably early in the morning, but he doubted if they'd attack yet because they knew the white men were armed with repeating rifles and able to resist.

Suddenly he sat up straight. Why the hell hadn't he thought of it before? The Utes had horses, six of them. Maybe they wouldn't attack as long as they thought the whites capable of fighting back successfully. But what if the white men were helpless, or if they seemed to be?

He said, "Sam. Cal. Flora. I've got an idea." Quickly he outlined his plans for them. Sam Joseph chuckled, then said in his deep, drawling voice, "You got it, Mr. Dolan. You got it this time. That's the only way we goin' to get horses, 'way out here."

Dolan asked, "What do you think, Cal?"

Daybright said doubtfully. "It might work. But how are you going to explain it to the Indian Bureau? You're going to have to kill those six Utes to get their horses away from them."

Dolan said, "I won't have any trouble explaining it. We're not going to attack the Utes. They're going to attack us. We're just going to defend ourselves."

Daybright said, "I'm as anxious to get out of this as any of you are. But that's murder. You're talking about setting a trap and letting them walk into it."

Dolan glanced toward him, unable to see more than a vague, blurred shape. He felt an angry irritation. A little while ago Daybright had been trying to fix blame for their predicament. Now, again, he was fixing blame for something that hadn't even happened yet.

Daybright said, "It's a matter of intent."

Dolan snorted disgustedly. "Damn it, Cal! Tell me what your intent was when you came along with this posse. You intended to kill the men that ran Susan down, didn't you?"

"I . . ."

"And what do you think those Utes intend to do to us if they get their way? They mean to kill us and capture Mrs. Doniphan."

"Maybe so. But . . ."

"Then don't talk to me about intent. We have a choice. Either we set a trap for those Utes and save our lives, or we wait until we're helpless and let them kill us then. Which do you want to do, Mr. Daybright? Or is it just that you want the blood to be on somebody else's hands?"

"You've got no right to talk to me that way."

"Haven't I? Consider the alternative to doing what I suggest. Either you keep up or we leave you behind. If you do keep up, you probably will die. If you get left behind, the Utes will kill you. Not much of a choice is it?"

"I guess it's not." Daybright's voice was sullen now.

"Then shut up about the morality of what we're going to do. If it makes the rest of you feel any better, I'll take full responsibility for it."

Sam Joseph said, "Sheriff, I think what you're goin' to do is right. I think it's the only chance we got."

"All right then. We'll rest here until it gets light. We'll leave Aragon's rifle behind, without cartridges, when we move on. That will convince 'em we're almost finished, if anything can. And we'll leave all but one of the canteens."

Daybright made no further protest. Dolan laid back and closed his eyes again. Flora asked softly, "Do you think it's going to work?"

"It's got to."

"What if they don't pick up our trail?"

Dolan knew that if the Utes didn't pick up their trail then they probably all would die. Unless Sam Joseph could go on alone, reach the trading post and return with horses and water and food. But if Sam should find the trading post burned and all the horses gone . . .

He said firmly, "They'll pick up our trail. They couldn't have been far away when the sandstorm hit." He believed his own words, but he had to admit the possibility that the Utes had given up when they saw the approaching sandstorm, that they might have turned back toward the reservation from which they were fugitives.

Again he closed his eyes, conscious of Flora not far away. Sam Joseph breathed deeply and regularly. Daybright's breathing was quick and rasping, as if the argument with Dolan had started the pains in his chest again. Thank God for Sam Joseph, Dolan thought. Without him, continuing would be impossible.

He slept at last and awakened as dawn was graying the eastern sky. He laid still several moments, listening. He heard nothing, but taking no chances, he got up laboriously, as if every movement hurt. He went from Daybright to Flora, awakening them, cautioning them that they were to act as if they were very weak.

Sam Joseph was already awake. Dolan said softly,

"Sam, we've got to figure that they'll hit us at any time. Find the first cover you can because I'd just as soon not be out in the open when they do."

Sam nodded. Dolan said, "Take my canteen and pour it into yours. I'll get the other two." He hobbled to Flora and took her canteen. He got Daybright's, too, and carried both back to Sam Joseph, who poured the contents into his own. The result of combining all the water was a canteen less than half-full.

Dolan said, "All right, let's go. Make it look good, but don't overdo it."

Sam Joseph moved out first, shuffling along listlessly. Daybright obviously didn't have to feign weariness. Flora only had to stop pretending to be strong. Dolan brought up the rear, shuffling as listlessly as the Negro guide.

He did not turn his head, but his eyes were active anyway. For almost an hour they traveled, stopping many times to rest. The sun climbed relentlessly across the cloudless sky.

At each stop, Dolan scanned the surrounding desert, looking for a lift of dust, a faint movement that would betray the presence of the Utes.

Ahead, he now saw some rocks, a low escarpment rising above the level desert floor. He said, "That looks like a good place, Sam."

"That's what I'm headin' for."

"See anything?"

"Dust. Them Indians out there, Mr. Dolan. They less than half a mile away."

"You think they'll hit us soon?"

"They goin' to try hittin' us before we reach them rocks."

"We don't dare hurry or we'll give ourselves away."

"Don't have to, Mr. Dolan. There's a gully between us an' them there rocks. It'll be as good a cover as the rocks would be."

Sam Joseph was carrying his rifle in his right hand. Daybright's was slung over his shoulder. Dolan carried his by the barrel, the stock resting on his shoulder. Flora Doniphan was unarmed.

Daybright started to take his rifle off his shoulder, but Dolan cautioned sharply, "Don't do that, Cal. Don't let them think that we're on guard."

Daybright let his hand fall away from his gun. He turned his head to look around, and Dolan said, "Huh uh. Don't look back."

Now the minutes dragged. The rocks seemed, instead of getting closer, to get farther away. The gully seemed an impossible distance. Dolan wondered if they could reach it in time.

Sam Joseph began to sing in his deep melodious voice. The tune was "Swing Low, Sweet Chariot," but the words were. "They comin', Mistuh Dolan, comin' 'bout a qua'tah mile behind. They just walkin' they hosses. I bet we goin' to reach that gully yet." He began to move a little faster, increasing his pace imperceptibly. Again, Daybright started to turn his head, but Dolan cautioned sharply, "Don't look back!"

A yell broke the silence, followed by other shrill yips and sudden thunder of horses' hoofs. Dolan yelled, "Run! Dammit, run!"

Sam Joseph was already running. Daybright broke into a run behind him, looking over his shoulder, his face white and scared. Flora began to run as Dolan came abreast of her. He reached out, took her hand, and pulled her along with him.

The gully was still a hundred yards away, and the Indians were less than three hundred yards behind. They'd never make it. Somehow, the Utes had to be slowed or stopped.

Dolan released Flora's hand and gave her a little shove. "Go on!"

He thought she might argue, might try to stay with

him. But she looked at his face, saw its expression and obeyed unquestioningly. Dolan whirled and knelt. He flung his rifle to his shoulder, watching with satisfaction the way the Utes veered aside out of respect for its accuracy. He fired, and the leading Utes' horse stumbled, fell and somersaulted heels over head, throwing his rider thirty feet. The Indian struck and rolled another twenty feet, raising a huge cloud of dust.

The others pulled up abruptly and scattered like quail to right and left. Glancing over his shoulder. Dolan saw that those ahead of him had reached the gully and disappeared.

He got up and ran, weaving from side to side in an effort to make it difficult for the Utes to draw a bead on him. He knew how accurate they were with the carbines they carried. He had been with Thornburgh during the Meeker Massacre.

Dust kicked up at his feet and immediately ahead. Suddenly Sam Joseph's face appeared over the lip of the gully. Smoke blossomed from the muzzle of Sam's rifle.

Dolan reached the gully and plunged into it. He gasped, "Let up, Sam. No more shooting. We don't want to scare them off."

Sam withdrew his rifle barrel. He peered through a clump of scrub brush on the gully's lip. "They havin' a powwow, Mr. Dolan."

"What about the one whose horse I shot?"

"He looks all right. Limpin' a little bit is all."

"You know Indians. What will they do now?"

Sam growled, "I know Cheyennes. They some diff'rent from Utes. But I figure they goin' to hold an' thirst an' heat. They got all the time in the world. They know we ain't."

"We can't wait. We've got to make them attack."

In a voice that was none too strong, Flora said, "They're after me, aren't they?"

Dolan nodded. "Yes."

"Then why not use me for bait? If I was to run away, staying close to the gully, they'd follow, wouldn't they?"

Dolan nodded again. "I expect they would."

"And the three of you could be right beside me but down out of sight in the gully. When I saw they were getting close, I could jump into the gully and you could shoot at them."

Dolan nodded. "It might work. Especially if one of us was to chase you and make it look like you were hysterical."

Daybright said, "I'll do that."

Dolan nodded. "All right. Sam and I will go on down the gully for a ways before you climb out of the ravine. Cal, let her stay maybe a hundred yards ahead."

Daybright nodded agreement. Dolan got up. He and Sam trotted down the ravine for a hundred yards. Dolan called, "Wait until I tell you, Flora."

Her face was gray, her eyes terrified. Dolan called reassuringly, "It will be all right. We'll be near."

She nodded wordlessly. Dolan called, "All right, Flora. Now."

She climbed the precipitous side of the ravine with some difficulty because of her long skirts. But she made it and paused on the lip of the gully on hands and knees a moment before she got to her feet.

She began to run now, looking back with unfeigned terror at the mounted Indians. The one whose horse had been killed swung up behind one of the others, and with shrill yells, the six came after her, galloping.

Dolan and Sam moved along the gully, keeping ahead, catching occasional glimpses of Flora's dress. Dolan yelled, "Daybright! Now!"

Daybright climbed out of the ravine, looked

around, then got up and ran after Flora, yelling at
her to come back. She kept running. The hoofs of the
Utes' ponies made a rumbling thunder in the air.

Flora veered close to the gully, now less than fifty
feet behind Dolan and Sam. She panted, "They're
getting awfully close!"

"Have they caught up with Daybright yet?"

"They've passed him. He dived back into the
gully."

"Then drop! Flat! Now!"

She obeyed instantly and unquestioningly. Dolan
and Sam scrambled up the steep gully side, poked
their heads above the level of the plain and shoved
the rifle muzzles ahead of them.

Flora rolled to avoid one of the Indians, who was
leaning far to one side, reaching out for her. Dolan
fired, and the Indian pitched off the side of his horse,
rolled fifteen feet beyond where Flora was and afterward lay still.

Sam shot a second one, who slumped over his
horse's withers, clinging, hanging on with his ebbing
sparks of life. Dolan saw a third swing to the ground
just short of where Flora lay and come running
toward her. The Ute knew by now that he and his
companions had ridden into a trap. His steel toma-
hawk was raised, and Dolan saw that he meant to kill
Flora Doniphan with it.

He took a careful bead on the Indian's chest,
pulled ahead a little and fired, afterward holding his
breath because he knew that if he had missed there
would be no time for a second shot. But he hadn't
missed. The Ute pitched forward, fell, rolled and
ended up practically at Flora's feet.

Dolan yelled, "Flora! Over here! Get down in the
gully!"

She got up instantly and ran. She stumbled on her
skirt and fell but got up again. She plunged into the

gully as if she was diving into a lake, rolled to the
bottom and stopped in a rising cloud of dust. Dolan
didn't know if she was hurt or not, and there wasn't
time to find out. He fired at another Indian, missed
and fired a second time. The Indian tumbled off his
horse on the far side, dragged briefly as he clung to
the reins, then lay limp and dead in a dust cloud
when he let go.

Four of the six Utes now were dead. Only the two
riding double were left. Sam's rifle roared, and one of
the two slumped forward, held erect now by the one
riding behind him. The horse veered away, and the
remaining Ute drummed frantically on the horse's
sides with his heels.

Dolan said, "Sam, you'll be better at this than I
would. Get up there and catch one of those horses, so
we can round the others up."

Sam crawled carefully up out of the ravine. Slowly,
talking in a low monotone, he approached the
nearest horse.

The animal moved away nervously. Sam circled,
until he was downwind from the animal. Still talking
soothingly, now in the Cheyenne tongue, he continued to approach. The horse continued to edge away.

Sam followed patiently for more than two hundred
yards. In the end, he got close enough to grasp the
horse's reins. Having done so, he jumped to the
horse's back and rode away at a trot to round up the
other three.

Dolan helped Flora out of the gully. She was
shaken and bruised but not hurt seriously.

He put his arms out and drew her close to him. She
wept wildly and hysterically for a long, long while.
Even after she had stopped, she still sobbed occasionally, the way a child sometimes will. Dolan looked
down and said simply, "Flora Doniphan, your husband was certainly a fool."

CHAPTER NINETEEN

ALL DAY THEY rode through the baking desert heat. Sam Joseph still led. Daybright followed him. Dolan brought up the rear, following Flora Doniphan.

Her face and neck were sunburned cruelly. There were abrasions on both her face and arms from the fall to the gully floor. She was obviously near exhaustion, both emotionally and physically. But she did not complain.

Near sundown, Sam Joseph pointed ahead, and Dolan, staring intently in the direction he was pointing, saw what he had feared he might, a faint wisp of smoke lifting on the horizon. Sam Joseph said, "That's McGuffy's Trading Post."

"How far away is it?"

"Five miles, I reckon. What's left of it."

"You don't think we could be closer, and that could be smoke from a cooking fire?"

"Huh uh. That ain't no cook fire, Mr. Dolan."

Sam lifted his horse to a trot, and the others followed suit. Steadily they drew nearer until at last they could see the trading post ahead. The building itself was a pile of blackened embers. Nearby was a corral, empty, the gate standing open.

Dolan could make out two bodies lying between the burned-out trading-post building and the corral.

At the edge of the yard he rode past Flora saying, "Wait here. It won't be a pleasant sight."

Daybright rode ahead of him, following the tracker, Sam. The heat from the embers of the building was intense.

Two bodies lay close to the corral. Dolan had never seen either one, but he knew who they were. The bank robbers, the outlaws they had been pursuing all this time.

There was another body of a man in his fifties, bearded and powerful, near the smoking ruin of the post. Dolan looked questioningly at Sam. "McGuffy?"

"Yes, sir. That's McGuffy."

Dolan said, "Scout around. Pick up Aragon's trail."

Sam obediently rode away to make a circle of the place. Dolan beckoned Daybright and Flora and then rode to the small trickle at the edge of the corral. He let his Indian pony drink, but the horse was not very thirsty, indicating the Utes had experienced no trouble finding water.

Sam Joseph yelled. "Got it, Mr. Dolan!"

Dolan looked at Flora. "I'm sorry. We can't stop to rest. We can't even take time to bury these bodies."

"It's all right."

Dolan yelled at Sam. "Come back and water your horse and fill that canteen."

Sam rode back toward him. Dolan dismounted, saying to Flora and Daybright, "Get yourselves a good drink before we leave."

Daybright dismounted and lay prone at the side of the little stream. He sucked up the water noisily, the way the horses had. Dolan did the same. Flora looked at both men doubtfully, then lay prone herself and drank. She was smiling at her own ineptness as she rose.

When they had finished drinking, Sam Joseph re-filled the canteen. He hung it from the saddle horn.

He laid down and drank, allowed his horse to drink, then mounted up and rode to where he had found the trail. Dolan caught up. He stared down at the trail. "Don't look like they're hurrying."

Sam shook his head. "Huh uh, Mr. Dolan. They ain't hurryin'. They figure we done for back there someplace. They figure they in the clear."

"How old is the trail?"

"Six hours."

"All right. We'll go as long as you can see the trail."

Sam rode at a steady trot. The trading post and the lifting wisp of smoke became invisible behind. Light faded from the high clouds, and gray crept across the land. At last, in almost total darkness, Sam Joseph pulled his Indian pony to a halt. "Can't see it no more, Mr. Dolan."

Dolan dismounted, went back and helped Flora to dismount. He held her a moment to steady her, and she seemed glad to have him do so. Daybright collapsed to the ground with a groan. Dolan said sharply, "Hang onto your horse's reins, Mr. Daybright. Don't let him go."

He fumed at the thought of wasting the whole night here, because he was now pursuing more than a couple of bank robbers. He was pursuing sworn possemen who had turned bad, who had murdered wantonly. He said, "Sam, go on for a few miles. If they're so damn sure they're safe, they might be foolish enough to have a fire."

"Yes, sir. I was thinkin' that." Sam rode away.

Dolan said, "Lie down, Flora, and try to rest."

She did so obediently. Dolan sat down beside her and took the reins of her horse from her. Daybright spoke from the darkness, bitterly, "Susan's dead, and the three men who killed her are dead, and all of a sudden I feel like everything's just drained out of me.

It's like there wasn't any sense to it, like there was nothing left."

Dolan didn't say anything immediately. He knew how Daybright felt. He had sometimes felt that way himself. At last he said, "The law is left, Mr. Daybright." It sounded lame and he doubted if it was any comfort to Daybright but he knew, if Daybright did not, that each time the law was upheld and enforced it became stronger. Each time it was defeated it became weaker. He supposed that was why catching Aragon, Grogan and Sims was so vitally important to him now.

None of the three could sleep. An hour passed, another and another still.

At last Dolan heard Sam Joseph's horse returning. He called out, "Sam!"

Sam rode to him and dismounted stiffly. "Found 'em, Mr. Dolan, an' you was right. They got a big cook fire. They got some whisky, too."

Dolan got to his feet and helped Flora up. He boosted her onto her horse and mounted up himself. Daybright was slow mounting, but he caught up before they had gone a hundred yards.

For an hour and a half they rode without stopping. Nobody spoke. The only sounds were those of the Indian ponies' unshod hoofs.

At last Sam Joseph stopped at the crest of a shallow rise. He pointed ahead, and Dolan saw the faint winking of firelight in the distance, a mere pinprick against the vast blackness of the desert. Sam went on, and for another half hour they rode, before Sam halted a second time. They were now like more than a hundred yards from the blazing fire, which the three fugitives had built in a little grove of willows and cottonwoods on the bank of a dry streambed.

Dolan whispered, "Where are their horses, Sam?"

"Far side of camp. Tied up in the trees."

"Circle around and get them. Lead them off a quarter mile or so and tie them up again. We'll need them going back."

Sam disappeared into the darkness. Dolan, Daybright and Flora Doniphan waited impatiently. Sam was gone half an hour. When he returned he said softly, "They safe now, Mr. Dolan."

"All right. Dismount and tie the horses here. Flora, you stay with them. Sam—Cal—Let's move in quiet now. If we get the drop on them, we may be able to take them without having to kill anyone."

He and the others moved silently toward the camp. Sims and Grogan were having an argument. Aragon was staring into the fire, a bottle in his hand. None of the three were really drunk yet, Dolan saw.

Aragon turned and snarled at the other two, "For Christ's sake, shut up! I'm sick of listening!"

Grogan and Sims turned their heads to stare at him resentfully. Dolan, Sam and Daybright were now less than a hundred feet away, still hidden by darkness. Dolan motioned for Sam Joseph to circle and come in from the other side. He watched Sam leave, silent for a man so big. He gave him enough time to make the circle, then jacked a cartridge into his rifle with a sound that shocked the three men at the fire into immobility. Dolan said, "That's fine, boys. Just hold real still, and nobody will get hurt."

Aragon was the first to move. He flung himself sideways off the rock, grabbing for the revolver in his holster as he rolled.

Dolan leveled the rifle, waiting until Aragon's movement would stop, until he could fire a crippling shot. He didn't want Aragon killed if it could be helped.

Aragon stopped rolling, leveled the revolver and fired at Dolan, whom he now could see in the firelight. Dolan felt something strike him on the head

and briefly saw flashing lights before his eyes. He had
a sensation of falling and felt his face dig itself into
the dirt. He heard a terrified cry from out in the
darkness, Flora's voice, "No! Oh my God. . . ."

Consciousness hung elusively, close to his grasp but
just beyond. He fought to regain it, and did, to hear
gunfire crackling. Above his head, Daybright's rifle
was booming out, and across the fire, Sam Joseph's
was also firing. Dolan brought himself to his hands
and knees in time to see Grogan double over, hugging his belly with both arms. Blood was running
over Grogan's bare forearms and dripping to the
ground.

Sims slammed back, struck in the chest. He fell,
part of him in the fire, and had enough life left to utter one terrible, agonizing scream. Hair and flesh
burned and filled the air near the fire with its stench.

Dolan couldn't see Aragon. He found his voice and
yelled, "Where's Aragon? Damn it, where's Aragon?"

But he didn't have to ask. He knew. Flora had
screamed as he was hit and had given her location
away. He yelled, "Flora? Are you all right?"

His answer came from Aragon, behind in the
darkness where the horses had been tied, where Flora
was. "So far she is! But by God, if any of you moves,
I'll cut her throat!"

Dolan yelled, "Flora?" wanting to hear from her,
unwilling to believe that Aragon had captured her.

His answer was plain enough. It was not words but
a sudden, hysterical weeping from Flora Doniphan.
And then she found her voice enough to cry, "I
thought you had been killed!"

Aragon called, "I'm taking her. Just stand still, all
of you, and she'll stay alive."

Dolan knew that was a lie. His thoughts were still
confused and his head ached ferociously, but he knew
that was a lie. Aragon couldn't let Flora live. He'd

have to kill her outright or abandon her someplace, because alive, she could and would put a noose around his neck.

Suddenly he broke and ran, straight toward Aragon. Running, he yelled, "Sam! Daybright! Rush him!"

Flame speared toward him from the darkness where the horses were. He heard Aragon curse savagely and heard the sound of a fist striking flesh and bone. Flame speared toward him again, and this time he felt a searing burn along his upper thigh.

He stumbled over Flora Doniphan, whom Aragon had struck and knocked down with his fist. He plunged forward, balance gone, and hit Aragon's legs with his shoulders as he fell.

Aragon's gun discharged again, its concussion deafening. But the man was falling even as he fired it, his legs knocked out from under him by Dolan's shoulder striking them. He threw out his hands to break his fall. Sitting there, clearly illuminated by firelight, he was vulnerable, and Dolan could have shot him dead. Instead, Dolan struggled to his feet, took three steps forward and jabbed the gun muzzle viciously into Aragon's back. "Move and I'll blow a hole in you big enough to stick my arm through."

Aragon froze, motionless. Dolan said, "Get up, but leave the gun right there on the ground."

Aragon obeyed. Sam Joseph and Daybright arrived, panting and out of breath. Dolan said, "Stick your gun muzzle in his ribs, Sam, while I put the handcuffs on him."

He yanked Aragon's wrists around behind his back, one by one, and snapped the handcuffs on. He threw the key out into the darkness, saying with savage satisfaction, "It'll take a blacksmith to get them off you, Floyd."

He was now so weary he could hardly stand. He

staggered to the fire and sat down heavily. He picked up the bottle of whisky Aragon had been drinking from. He took a long drink. He was remembering the tone in Flora's voice, screaming as he went down. She came to him now, a dampened cloth in her hand, to carefully wash the wound on the side of his head. Sam Joseph was going through Aragon's saddlebags. He called, "They full of money, Mr. Dolan. They just plumb full of money."

Dolan said wearily, "Bury Grogan and Sims. We'll rest a couple of hours and then start back."

Flora's hands were gentle, and she was looking at him in a way that made him feel ten feet tall. His head ached and his thigh hurt, but the pain was bearable.

In him now was a deep feeling of satisfaction, one he hadn't known in years. The law had been upheld. He had almost forgotten how satisfying that could be.

He said, "You watch him, Sam," and laid down on the warm ground at the fire's side. He was almost instantly asleep, but even as he drifted off he knew Flora Doniphan would be there beside him when he awoke.

Lewis B. Patten wrote more than ninety Western novels in thirty years and three of them won Spur Awards from the Western Writers of America and the author himself the Golden Saddleman Award. Indeed, this highlights the most remarkable aspect of his work: not that there is so much of it, but that so much of it is so fine. Patten was born in Denver, Colorado, and served in the U.S. Navy 1933–1937. He was educated at the University of Denver during the war years and became an auditor for the Colorado Department of Revenue during the 1940s. It was in this period that he began contributing significantly to Western pulp magazines, fiction that was from the beginning fresh and unique and revealed Patten's lifelong concern with the sociological and psychological effects of group psychology on the frontier. He became a professional writer at the time of his first novel, *Massacre at White River* (1952). The dominant theme in much of his fiction is the notion of justice, and its opposite, injustice. In his first novel it has to do with exploitation of the Ute Indians, but as he matured as a writer he explored this theme with significant and poignant detail in small towns throughout the early West. Crimes, such as rape or lynching, were often at the centre of his stories. When the values embodied in these small towns are examined closely, they are found to be wanting. Conformity is always easier than taking a stand. Yet, in Patten's view of the American West, there is usually a man or a woman who refuses to conform. Among his finest titles, always a difficult choice, surely are *A Killing at Kiowa* (1972), *Ride a Crooked Trail* (1976), and his many fine contributions to Doubleday's Double D series, including *Villa's Rifles* (1977), *The Law at Cottonwood* (1978), and *Death Rides a Black Horse* (1978). His later books include *Tincup in the Storm Country* (1996), *Trail to Vicksburg* (1997), *Death Rides the Denver Stage* (1999), and *The Woman at Ox-Yoke* (2000).

.